Mike Edwards began, "First, I want an island, under the tightest security, where we can stash a half-dozen or so prominent people for a year or two."

"An island!"

"Next, I want you to round up the dozen or so most prominent scholars of comparative religion."

"But—"

"Then I want a seminary," Mike added.

"A what!"

"A seminary." Mike continued, "Then I want the computers to go through the dossiers of everyone in the country who has an I.Q. over 125, and can speak Russian."

The CIA man looked at Edwards in dismay. "What in hell is all this *for?*"

"For the new missionary seminary of the Old Time Religion Church, of course."

World traveler, expert observer of the human condition, Mack Reynolds has been a world famous Science Fiction writer for more than two decades. In fact, of all the writers published in the leading SF magazines, *Galaxy* and *If*, a poll conducted among the readers put the stories of Mack Reynolds consistently higher than any other. Perhaps it is because his stories have an uncanny way of discussing now the questions that will concern everyone ten or twenty years later.

Mack Reynolds is the author of more than two hundred SF short stories, novelettes and novels. Many of them have been published by Ace Books and more will be published in future months.

Mack Reynolds has written the following Ace books:

BLACKMAN'S BURDEN
BORDER, BREED NOR BIRTH
CODE DUELLO
COMPUTER WAR
DAWNMAN PLANET
DEPRESSION OR BUST
LOOKING BACKWARD FROM THE YEAR 2000
MERCENARY FROM TOMORROW
PLANETARY AGENT X
THE RIVAL RIGELLIANS
SATELLITE CITY
THE SPACE BARBARIANS
AMAZON PLANET

TOMORROW MIGHT BE DIFFERENT

by

Mack Reynolds

ace books
A Division of Charter Communications Inc.
1120 Avenue of the Americas
New York, N.Y. 10036

TOMORROW MIGHT BE DIFFERENT

An ACE BOOK

A shorter version of this novel was published in *The Magazine of Fantasy and Science Fiction* under the title RUSSKIES GO HOME! and has also been reprinted abroad.

Printed in U.S.A.

I

Mike Edwards plowed his way through the dazzling white sand towards the Russkie party as quickly as he could.

"Just a moment, Miss," he called out in Russian. "Just a moment, please!" Hurrying was difficult, he was in ordinary dress and wore shoes, rather than beachwear.

One of the girls, the very attractive one, had come onto the beach in a robe, one of the flamboyant new textiles the Russians were producing that all but knocked your eyes out. It was his private opinion that the Russian taste was all in their mouth; but, then, that had applied since the days of the Czars.

It was when she had slipped out of her robe that Mike's eyes had popped. Her tiny trunks left nothing whatsoever to the imagination, but that wasn't it. She wore no top at all. It would have been hard for her to be any more naked.

Surfeited with womanhood as Mike was in the tourist season, he still had to admit that she made a striking appearance indeed, not too big, not too small, youthfully firm, a body just short of lush, and her nipples were coral pink. . . . But this was Spain!

He came closer and said, anxiously apologetic, "Look here, Miss——"

She was frowning questioningly at him, no more self-conscious than a two year old in its bath. "Saratov," she said. "Catherina Saratov."

She took him in. What she saw was a rather gangly man in his early thirties, pleasant of face, though it was now somewhat anxious; rumpled of hair, which was brown; dark blue of eyes, which were somewhat on the sincere and worried side; six feet tall, about one hundred and sixty-five.

Mike Edwards placed her vaguely. In his position, it was absolutely impossible to learn the names of all of his charges. They came for periods running from two weeks to a month, seldom longer, and in a season's time, he had literally thousands on his hands. However, they had sat at the same table at a Horizonal Holidays party the other night. He had thought, even then, that she was the epitome of Slavic beauty. The ultra-blondness, just short of platinum blonde (but natural), fair-skinned as only the very northern people are fair skinned, impossibly blue-eyed, excellent carriage, as though she had been ballet trained, and without the heft of the average Russkie. Contrary to much popular opinion, the Russian is a blonde rather than a brunette and when a Russian is beautiful there is nothing to surpass her in the Caucasian world.

Mike cleared his throat, again apologetically, and said, "Look, Miss Saratov, this is Spain. Catholic, you know, and very conservative. Except for Portugal, there's probably no more conservative country in Common Europe."

"Oh," she said, still somewhat puzzled. "You must mean my bathing suit."

"Well, yes, in a way. It's very pretty, of course. Very chic, but. . . ." He let his sentence dribble away, tried to keep from letting his eyes leave her face and descend to the delicious looking semi-globes; decided it was obvious that he was doing so and did a fair job of blushing. What was the old term? She was really stacked. Mike Edwards had always been a tit man.

Catherina Saratov said, "But everybody wears this type of suit on the Crimea beaches now. It is so very comfortable when swimming and one can achieve a much better tan."

"I'm sure," Mike said, nodding in support of her statement. "But this is Torremolinos and the Spanish are most conservative. Their authorities insist. It is part of their religion. Modesty, you know, and all that."

"Oh well, of course," she said. "If it is their religion. One mustn't ignore religious customs in a foreign country. It would be uncultured."

She very prettily stooped and took up a table napkin from one of the picnic baskets and did some things with it deftly, wrapping it around her upper body. "Religious customs are fascinating."

Mike sighed, cleared his throat again and said, "Sorry to bother you, Miss Saratov. How are you and your party enjoying yourselves? Is there anything I can do? Are your suites comfortable? The food satisfactory?"

The other Russkies in the group had been busy with their own beach preparations. Now one of them, a beefy forty-year old with a red face and a bushy untrimmed mustache, who looked like he already had a half dozen drinks this morning, came up. He introduced himself as Nicholas Galushko and shook hands—they always shook hands. Mike Edwards estimated that he got his damn hand shaken a thousand times an average day. They shook hands every time they met you, even if this happened ten times in a single hour.

Nicholas Galushko said to Mike complainingly, "It's too hot. This Spanish sun is too hot. Why aren't the beaches here air-conditioned? In the Black Sea resorts all the beaches are air-conditioned. In your Horizontal Holidays advertisements in *Pravda* you didn't mention that the beaches weren't air-conditioned."

"Well," Mike said placatingly, "that's the way it goes. Some countries haven't gotten to the point of air-conditioning beaches as yet. That's the reason some people come to Spain, to see the things as they were in the old days. Very primitive, I imagine, by your standards."

One of the other Russkies, a stocky woman in her mid-thirties, as far opposite to Catherina Saratov in physical attractiveness as possible, came up and shook hands with Mike and introduced herself as Ana Chekova, She evidently didn't wear the type of bathing suit that Catherina did because she knew better. She got in on the complaints. "All of our beaches are air-conditioned and up on the Arctic Ocean the beaches in Siberia are warmed with ultra-violet rays."

Mike inwardly winced at some of the economic ramifications of that, but continued his genial smile as became the position he held. "I'd like to visit the Soviet Complex some day," he said.

"Why don't you, Comrade?" Catherina smiled at him. "You've heard about the new policy for foreign tourists, haven't you?"

He was a tourist agent and got most of the international publications on the subject, but this was something new. He said, in spite of a premonition of disaster, "I don't think so. What new policy?"

"It's free."

"Free?" Mike said blankly.

She nodded. "You have to pay your own expenses up to the border, of course, but once in the Soviet Complex all costs are borne by the State. It's for good will. In the old days we had, what is your Americanism? a bad image. So to change that we invite the world to visit us. All for the good will."

For a moment, Mike let his mind reel with the implications and its effect on such companies as his employers, Horizonal Holidays, based in England. But then he decided he'd better leave it for a more tranquil moment—sometime, perhaps when he was safely in bed and it could drive him to insomnia, or better, to an overdose of sleeping pills.

Galushko had popped open a bottle of the Spanish champagne they'd brought in their portable refrigerator and was pouring a glass. He sipped it, making a face. "Not up to our Armenian champagne," he scowled. He looked accusingly at Mike. "This Spanish champagne is second rate, not sweet enough."

Mike said, "Well, that's the way it goes. Different countries, different tastes. Most of the Western countries like their champagne very dry, *brut*. As a matter of fact, the Spanish champagne is sweeter than French."

"Dry champagne," Galushko scoffed. "No taste!"

Mike said hopefully, "Well, if you will all excuse me, I'll get about my rounds."

Galushko was having none of that. "Oh, have a glass of the wine," the Russkie said overbearingly.

Mike said, knowing that it was a losing battle, "Well, I

don't like to start drinking until after lunch, at least. I have a hard day in front of me, you know."

"Oh, come on. Drink! Enjoy yourself. Life is short. And what is better than food and drink? Here try this. Caviar from the Caspian. Real caviar! Not the mush you foreigners eat. We're expanding a hundred fold the sturgeon beds—the new plan is to produce eighteen times as much fresh caviar."

He pushed a still foaming glass of wine into Mike's right hand, pressed a large chunk of dark bread deeply covered with gray beluga caviar into his left.

Here we go again, Mike sighed inwardly. Surely this season would end with liver trouble, not to speak of ulcers.

However, Catherina Saratov smiled at him and that was something. She had the kind of smile that looked as though she meant it. Anybody can smile—kind of. He could feel hers go deep down within, something he hadn't thought possible in mid tourist season.

He let Galushko refill his glass and watched as the girl dashed for the water. Her buttocks were as interesting as had been her bosom. He wouldn't mind getting into that. He wondered if he would have a chance. She didn't particularly seem to have a man in tow.

II

When Mike Edwards was able to escape, he made his way over to the escalator that took you up from the Mediterranean beach to the miramar near the old Moorish tower which originally gave the formerly small fishing village its name. It was, for all practical purposes, all that remained of the once art colony, save a couple of blocks about the town plaza. Today, Torremolinos was one of the largest resorts on the Costa del Sol of Spain, which stretched from Malaga to Gibraltar, and accommodated hundreds of thousands of visitors each year—especially Russkies.

He went on up Calle San Miguel, teeming with its tourist shoppers, and made his way to the Espadon Hotel. That afternoon he was going to have to line up some of his hundreds of clients for a side trip to Granada and the sightseeing tour of the Alhambra. He didn't look forward to it. The first few dozen times weren't so bad, but when you've gone through the Alhambra on several hundred occasions you got to hating the Moors as much as Ferdinand and Isobel must have.

He was still slightly light-headed from the unaccustomed drinking of cold champagne under the broiling Spanish sun with no more on his stomach than the Continental breakfast of coffee, hard roll, butter and marmalade. He had got away after three glasses, about par for the course when a Russkie caught you. He wondered how in the devil they could keep up the pace.

He stopped off at the main bar for a Fernet Branca in hopes of settling his stomach, got up on a stool and gave Manuel his order.

On the stool next to him sat another of his clients, this one an American, if Mike remembered correctly. He prayed inwardly and hopelessly that the other would leave him alone. He might as well have prayed for rain on the moon.

The other said, "How's it going, Mr. Edwards? I don't exactly envy you your job."

Mike said, "Just fine. Lovely weather, isn't it?"

The other said, "You've probably forgotten my name. I'm Frank Jones, from SanSan, California."

"Of course not," Mike lied. "You came on the plane from London, on Friday." Actually, he did remember Mr. Jones, although not by name. The man stood out due to his lack of typicalness. The other tourists came in sportswear, most of them bearing cameras, skin diving apparatus, tennis tackets, golf clubs and such. Mr. Jones had landed in a business suit, in which he was presently sweltering and was looking glum even as vacationists went. He had a sad face, somewhat reminiscent of Lincoln before he grew the beard, must have gone about forty years of age, but was seemingly in good physical trim. He was nursing a bottle of beer.

Mike said, "SanSan? That doesn't tell you much. The city stretches from San Francisco to San Diego now, doesn't it."

"I come from the area once known as Santa Barbara," Jones said.

Automatically, Mike let his eyes go around the bar, checking to see if any of his people were in some kind of a bind. Two or three of the Russkies were taking shots in the patio-lounge with their 3-D cameras. Regardless of country, the tourist is a snapshot taker, but no nation on earth had ever equalled the Russkies.

Just to be saying something, Mike said, "I wonder why none of the Western countries have ever gone into producing 3-D cameras. It's a natural development in photography."

Frank Jones snorted his dour indignation. "How? With the Russkies flooding the market with their product at five dollars per camera, retail, how would a Western company ever get going? That Mikoyan Camera works up in Leningrad has a capacity as high as all other camera factories in the world combined. All automated, of course. I understand that less than a hundred men are employed in the place. Basically, it turns out cameras for the Soviet Complex, but when the Kremlin decides it needs some foreign exchange, they dump a couple of hundred million cameras on the world market at cutthroat prices."

"I guess you're right," Mike said. "Where will it end? They're selling aircushion cars all over Europe for about two hundred dollars. I understand that Volkswagen-Fiat is thinking of folding up. Can't stand the competition. Of course," he added loyally, "I don't think they're up to the standards of the Ford-Chevrolet Company, cars, but . . . ."

"But two hundred bucks is a far cry from four thousand," Jones finished. "It gets to the point where if you need some minor repairs, you don't bother. You throw the car away and buy another one."

"It piles up," Mike agreed.

"In actuality, it's the same deal as with the cameras," Jones pursued. "Back in the 1960s the Russkies didn't turn out more than a few thousand automobiles a year. They were interested in building more steel mills, more basic industry. But when they got to the point where they were producing all the steel they could possibly use, in the 1970s, they built an automated automobile plant, there in Sverdlovak, that dwarfed anything the rest of the world had ever seen."

Mike shifted uncomfortably on his stool, but he couldn't leave in the middle of the other's conversation. He didn't particularly go in for such subjects these days. People came down here to relax, not to dwell on the ulcer breeding economics of the world.

Jones was saying, "Not an obsolete piece of machinery in the plant. No worry about competition, either. A captive market of a couple of billion people, if you count the Chinese. No need to change designs every year to attract buyers. At least a twenty-five million car a year capacity, in that one plant alone. No wonder they can afford to sell them for two hundred dollars."

Catherina Saratov came strolling into the patio-lounge done up in the latest from Budapest, the Soviet Complex style center, a shimmering disposable material now being turned out by the billions of yards. Mike watched her cross the room. She moved as a professional dancer moves, graceful, confident. It hit him all over again. Holy smokes but the girl was attractive. He felt a stirring within him.

He turned to his companion, and interrupted. "You'll

have to pardon me," he said. "One of my clients that I have to check with, just entered."

"Sure," Jones said, although he seemed to dislike the idea of Mike leaving.

Mike got off the stool and headed for the girl, racking his mind for something to say to her. Some excuse for his accosting her.

III

The next day, Mike Edwards was scheduled to take a party to Malaga, eight miles north of Torremolinos, for a bullfight. It was in the way of being something special. The aging Manola Segura had come out of retirement for the third time and was having a series of *mano a mano* corridas with Carlos Arruza 3rd.

Mike's party consisted of seventy Horizonal Holidays tourists, sixty-five of them Russkies. He got his cut through the ticket purchases, buying in a block. Horizonal Holidays didn't mind such little rackets; they enabled the company to pay their agents minimum salaries. Mike had the nightclub tours, the tour to Granada, the tour to Gibraltar, the tour to Tangier, beach parties, and so forth. He made enough through the season, by this means, to last him throughout the year.

The road to Malaga was packed with cars and buses coming up from Torremolinos, Marbella, Estepona and probably, for such a fight as this, from as far as Gibraltar. Even if there had been more than a handful of Spanish *aficionados* who could afford the admission price, it looked improbable that they could have found seats in the bull plaza.

The Russkies, as always, were jubilant. Even on the way into town in the bus, the bubbling wine bottles went from hand to hand, laughter and jibes filled the interior, not to speak of raucous songs.

Mike stood, up next to the suffering driver. He had tried to wiggle into the seat next to Catherina Saratov but had missed out to a hulking Russkie pushing seven feet in height who looked more like a Turk than a Slav. A really brawny specimen, with shaved head, he must have gone almost 300 pounds. He had a ring of lard around the back of his neck, but he was far from fat otherwise. Now he had a magnum of champagne in one hand, a pair of castanets in the other. He was regaling all with a Russianized version of gypsy flamenco which made Mike inwardly wince—he was a flamenco lover, but was joyously received by the other's fellow countrymen, including Catherina.

One of the Russkies leaned far out a window and pointed excitedly. "Look, a car with wheels. Four wheels. How quaint. Look everybody!" She whipped up her camera for a shot and so did a dozen of the others.

Mike closed his eyes in pain.

Ana Chekova, the woman who had been with Catherina on the beach the day before, demanded of Mike, "Why do they still use land cars here? In the Soviet Complex, everyone uses aircushion cars. Automated aircushion cars. Much more comfortable and much safer. It's ridiculous to use wheel cars. And here in Spain the roads are not even automated. Very dangerous."

Mike cleared his throat. "Well, in some countries, such as Spain, they haven't yet got around to acquiring aircushion cars the way you have in the Soviet Complex. Sometimes they can't afford to buy a new one. As a matter of fact, some people prefer them—in a way."

"Ha!" Ana Chekova snorted.

Mike shrugged. It was a Russkie characteristic that they couldn't believe everybody wouldn't adopt each and every Russian gadget, given the chance. He didn't know it but it was a characteristic his own people were famous for a few decades earlier.

When he had first come to Spain, Mike Edwards had rather liked the bullfight. In theory, he was morally opposed to it. In practice it gave him a vicarious thrill he'd never found in any other spectator sport—if you could call it a sport, and purists didn't. Since the coming of the Russkie tourist wave, however, something was lost. The pageant, the excitement of the knowledgeable aficionado, the electric feeling of the fiesta brava was gone. Now the stands were packed with first comers, more occupied with their bottles and their 3-D cameras, uncaring about the niceties of the spectacle going on below them.

Mike had arranged it this time. His seat was next to Catherina's and right at the edge of the barrera. As a matter of fact, he was rather keen to see the *mano a mano* competition between Segura and Arruza. Also, he was trying to analyze this feeling he had developed for the Russkie girl. This was new—especially in season. He grinned wryly to himself. Was it because she was such an exception? A girl who wasn't wildly pursuing. There was a preponderance of female over male tourists of two to one in Torremolinos and usually it was all a thirty year old tourist agent could do to fight them off. They all seemed to act like bitches in heat. More than once he had returned to his room to find a nude woman in his bed, patiently waiting. How they got in he never knew.

The bugle blew and the paseo began. The two matadors, followed by their cuadrillas, paraded across the ring toward the judge's box, to salute him in much the manner the gladiators of Rome had once called to their emperor. *We who are about to die, salute you!*

Catherina Saratov said to him, "Actually a very uncultured sport, this bull baiting. Is it allowed in England, as well?"

"Well, I don't believe so," Mike said. "Only in some of the Latin countries, I think. I'm an American, you know, not British."

"An American." She stared at him, fascinated. She leaned forward and said, "Do you mind if I ask you a question?"

"Of course not." Mike was disconcerted. Not only because of her sudden eagerness as she leaned toward him, but due to the fact that this dress was almost as revealing as her beach costume.

Catherina said, with a certain horrified fascination, "Have you ever helped lynch a Black?"

He might have known that was coming. He got it with every contingent of Russkies that came through. Mike said, "Well, no. Our authorities take a very dim view of such activities. I'm from the State of New Mexico, myself. I doubt if anybody's been lynched there since the days of Billy the Kid."

He decided to go a bit further than usual in his capacity as Horizonal Holiday's tour manager in Torremolinos. He said, "Do you mind if I ask you a question, in turn?"

"Why, of course not."

"Have you ever been purged?"

"I beg your pardon?"

"Well, I understand that Russians think Americans spend half their time lynching each other. On the other hand, the idea in the United States is that the Russian national sport is purging."

"Purging?" Catherina said. "I don't believe I understand." Then, "Oh, purging. You mean back in the 1930s between Stalin and the Old Bolsheviks."

Mike said dryly, "I understand that wasn't exactly the last time you had a political purge."

Catherina shrugged her shoulders, which only increased her decollete and brought a dryness of mouth to Mike Edwards, and her attention went back to the ring where Manola Segura was waiting for his first bull of the afternoon.

She said, "In the early days after the revolution when the Soviets were still very poor, everybody fought to get to the top, as man has in all societies down through the ages. Only the higher bureaucrats and a few others, such as the higher officers in the armies, some of the writers, artists and entertainers, were able to live well. But as production developed the competition to rise above everyone else slackened off. Finally, for decades now, there is an abundance of everything, so we no longer need fight among ourselves."

Manola Segura's peones were running the bull, dragging their capes behind them, letting the animal chase them to the burladero shelters. Their matador watched warily, noting how el toro hooked, learning his characteristics. This was crucial, it was necessary that he learn everything possible about his opponent.

Mike Edwards had to tear his eyes away from the girl. It was a more sensible answer than he had expected after she had pulled that old wheeze about lynching.

Manola Segura came out now and went through a series of half a dozen veronicas with the bull. Very passable veronicas they were too; a Segura specialty. From the few Spaniards in the tendidos came a scattering of *olés*. The Russkies weren't particularly impressed.

Catherina said, "Why do they cheer?"

Mike said, "Well, he did that very gracefully and allowed the bull's horns to come very close."

The bugle sounded and Manola Segura retreated as the picadores emerged for the second act of the production, the Tercio de Varas.

"Those bulls are not so very large," Nick Galushko complained after taking a healthy swig from his champagne bottle. He was seated directly behind Mike and Catherina.

Mike said agreeably, "Well, they aren't as big as they used to be in the old days, so I am told, but I still wouldn't want to be down there."

Catherina said, "Very uncultured."

Somebody above them passed down a half empty but still chill bottle of champagne. Catherina took a short swallow, passed the bottle to Mike and returned her attention to the fray below. Mike didn't particularly want it but he took the opportunity to make a bond between them even though it was as small as a shared drink. What in the world was getting into him with this Russkie wench? He felt like a lovelorn highschool boy.

The Spanish were yelling, "*Olé, olé!*" Manola Segura had performed a particularly well done *quite*, rescuing one of the picadores and his horse from the charging bull.

The bugle sounded again and the fight entered the Tercio de banderillas. In his youth Manola Segura had often placed his own, but today he sent out his peones for the job.

He did his best work in the Tercio de Muerte. No one in Spain was better with the muleta and sword than old

Manola Segura and he knew it. He went through a veritable tour de force in his faena winding up with two or three Manoletinas.

A few spectators who appreciated what was going on dissolved into loud olés and after a perfect kill, going in over the horns, Manola was awarded two ears and a tail. He paraded the ring, holding them up for the crowd's approval. The Spanish cheered and so did the few foreigners present who had a working knowledge of the fiesta brava. Monola's peones followed after him, tossing back the hats, the women's fans, the leather wine bottles, that were showered down in way of Spanish applause. The Russkies cheered too, waved their bottles at Manola as he went by, and snapped desperately with their 3-D cameras.

Catherina frowned at Mike who had been beating his hands together and making with the olés as fervently as any. She said, "How can you applaud such primitive bull-baiting?"

Mike knocked it off and said mildly, "Well, it was possibly the best bull fight I've seen in three years. Manola Segura is of the old school. You don't see them much any more. The newcomers don't take the risks. Their pay is sky high and they want to live to spend it."

"Uncultured," Catherina said disapprovingly.

The bugle sounded and Carlos Arruza's first bull came exploding from the toril doors.

"A calf!" Nick Galushko muttered from behind them.

Mike said over his shoulder, "That's a three-year-old *bos taurus ibericus*, Mr. Galushko. Specially bred for fighting for a thousand years and more. The Spanish consider them the most dangerous animal in the world."

"Ha! You should see our range cattle in the Kazakh People's Republic. Then you would see bulls."

"Well," Mike said agreeably, "I'm sure you have some king-size bulls in Siberia all right."

The peones were running Arruza's animal for him, making the burladero shelters in the nick of time.

Mike shot to his feet suddenly. "Holy smokes," he snapped. "What's he doing?"

The oversized Russkie who had sat next to Catherina on the bus, was climbing over the barrera, down into the ring, a bottle of champagne in one hand, a wide, idiotic grin on his face, his shaved head bearing a sheen of sweat in the Spanish sun.

One of the Spaniards seated to Mike's right gasped, "An *espontáneo.*"

The Russian Cossack reeled across the ring in the direction of the bull who seemed somewhat taken aback by this new invasion.

Mike shot an agonized look in the direction of the barrera where the matadors and their assistants were sheltered. No aid seemed to be forthcoming from that direction. "Can't somebody do something!" he yelled. It was all he needed, to have one of his charges gored to death while on vacation in Torremolinos.

Nick Galushko was laughing hugely. "Sit down, sit down. Have another drink. Vova's all right. He's a Cossack."

"I don't care if he's Rasputin," Mike snapped. "He's drunk and that's a fighting bull. It hasn't even been whittled down by the picadores yet."

The rest of the Russkies, all over the arena, were cheering and laughing, urging their half-drunken compatriot onward.

Catherina said unworriedly, "Don't mind about Vovo Chernozov. He's a cattleman from Kazakh. He knows all about cattle. Besides, he is a great wrestler—Turkoman style. Look at the size of him."

Galushko tried to press a bottle of vodka into Mike's hand. "Nothing can hurt Vovo. He's a monster."

The bull was charging. Mike Edwards tried to close his eyes. He had to open them again, in fascination.

The gigantic Cossack stood, his feet poised, for a moment. Just before impact he spun away, lithe in spite of his size. The bull wheeled, somewhat in the same manner as when the banderilleros were placing their darts. It turned too sharply, pulled itself into an awkward position.

The Cossack stepped closer, the heavy champagne bottle held by the neck. He brought it down in a crushing blow behind the bull's ear. The animal, dazed, stumbled forward two or three steps and then sank to its knees, where it continued to shake its head.

The Russians throughout the plaza roared with laughter.

Vovo grinned widely, put one foot on the bull's back and waved in drunken triumph to his supporters. He left the bull and began touring the ring as Manola Segura had done with his two ears and tail. As he went, the Russkies cheered thunderously, interspacing their vision of olés with raucous laughter.

Vovo passed the barerra where Manola Segura and Carlos Arruza stood dressed in their highly decorative *trajes de luces*, for a score of generations the multicolored traditional dress of the matador. He put his thumb to his nose and made an internationally recognized gesture.

The crowd roared again.

Except for the Spanish, who remained quiet. Unsmiling.

IV

Mike would have liked to have eaten alone that evening but it wasn't in the cards. He had to make his rounds of the hotels, listen to the complaints, try to soothe relationships between tourists and hotel managers. One of the big beefs about the Russkies was the fact that they seldom stayed put in the rooms assigned them. If the French had formerly had a reputation for promiscuity, it was nothing compared to this. During a one month vacation period, a Russkie wench might occupy as many as a dozen different rooms, if not more, spreading her favors about with true communistic sharing of the bounty.

Tonight it was the Santa Clara. He was lucky enough to draw a table with only one other person, a Russian from Kiev and an unusually mild one at that. Mike remembered him vaguely, automatically asked him how things were going and to his surprise, got no complaints. Mike was mollified. He seldom thought in terms of his tourists being happy about their stay in Torremolinos; he simply assumed, in view of the number of beefs that he received, that everybody hated the place almost as much as he did, now at the height of the season.

However, it couldn't last. During the fish course, *calamares en su tinta*, a Spanish specialty of squid prepared in its own ink, the Russkie said, "I understand you are an American, Mr. Edwards. You speak our language very well."

"I'm afraid I have a rather strong Ukrainian accent," Mike told him. "My principal teacher was from Kharkov. I took some courses at the University in New Mexico. All the American schools teach Russian now. Then, of course, I get a good deal of practice with a job like this. I speak more Russian, in my daily work, than I do either English or Spanish."

"And English is our second language in the Soviet Complex," the other told him. "How are things in America? I have heard that with the current, ah recession, unemployment is severe."

"Rolling readjustment," Mike told him. "Way back before the First World War they called them panics, but that was bad for morale so they changed it to the more gentle depression. But even that was too strong, so it became recession, and now it's evolved to rolling readjustment, whatever that means. Anyway, it's terrible. I'd estimate that a third to a half of the working force back in the States is unemployed."

"A third!" The Russian was shocked. "The starvation must be terrible."

"Starvation?" Mike said blankly. Then he remembered that he had run into this discussion before. "No," he said. "You Russkies, pardon me, Russians, seem to think that because there are tens of millions unemployed in America today that they're all starving. Actually, many of them never had it so good."

It was the Russian's turn to look blank.

Mike said, "Listen, even back in the 1930s depression the American standard of living as compared to the rest of the world, was fabulous. You've got to realize that the Soviet Complex didn't invent the production of abundance. We Americans did. We've had it for half a century and more. Right now, it's driving us batty. We don't know how to control it."

The Russian began, "But I've always been led to believe that it was the Seven Year Plan that was started in the early 1970s that first developed——"

Mike was waggling a finger negatively. "No, sir. If you insist I might go along with you on Ivan Ivanovitch or somebody or other inventing the steamboat, or Georgi Georgiovitch flying an airplane before the Wright brothers. However, I will not retreat an inch on the fact that we Americans first developed the production of superabundance. I'll also admit that we still have to figure out what to do with it all—but we were the first. You Russians have it too, now, and so has Common Europe, but we were fanny deep in agricultural surpluses, for instance, while you people were still eating black bread and cabbage in the way of diet."

"But the unemployed. You just admitted that there were tens of millions of unemployed."

"Yeah," Mike said. "The unemployed. Do you think that any office holder in the United States would remain there overnight if he voted for anything that involved *not* taking care of the unemployed? Once a month, at least, every politician in the country gets up on his hind legs and gives a blistering attack against the trend toward the Welfare State. It's expected of him, like being against sin and for mother and freedom. Then he goes back to his seat in Congress and votes another increase in the Guaranteed Annual Income, and every pension and veteran's bonus in sight."

The Russian was taken aback.

Mike snorted. "I know at least a couple of dozen young men back home who have never had a job in their lives. They live in suburban homes, drive their own cars, raise families, take vacation trips. Vacations yet. Vacations from what? What's more," he added glumly, "the way things look, they never *will* hold down a job—the new leisure class. With the advances in technology, it looks as though the United States will have another half million unemployed this year to add to last year's total."

The Russian said, "Well, why are you here? Why don't you go home and get a job being unemployed?"

"Damn it!" Mike roared. "Because I'm in revolt. I think people *ought* to work, even if it's only as meaningless a job as listening to the silly complaints of tourists. The world may get to the point where technology throws ninety-nine men out of a hundred out of work, but I'll find something to do if it kills me!"

"I'm a doctor," the Russian said soothingly. "If it affects you this strongly, it might."

"Might what?" Mike said, more calmly.

"Might kill you. You'll have a stroke. How about another vodka?"

"No thanks," Mike said. "I'm sorry, Doctor. I've had a hard day and that's my particular sore spot."

V

Mike Edwards wasn't making the progress he would have liked with Catherina. He didn't know why. He was so used to having women tourists fall all over him that it was hard to accept one who didn't respond at all. He spent his spare time hanging around the hotel where she was quartered for her Horizonal Holidays vacation.

It was there, in the main bar, that he ran into Frank Jones again. By this time, the other had acquired a sport shirt and had shed his suit coat, but he still didn't look like a typical Horizonal Holidays client and he still had his dour expression.

Mike said, automatically, "How goes the vacation?"

And Jones said, slowly, as though seeking for words, "Actually, Mr. Edwards, this isn't a vacation for me."

"What is it, then? Any way I can help?" He gave the patio-lounge a quick sweep with his eyes, but there was no sign of Catherina.

Frank Jones said, "I was sent to see how you were getting along with the Russkie tourists. First I was to size you up from a distance, and then approach you."

That brought Mike's eyes back to the other in a hurry. "By whom? And why? Who cares, except Horizontal Holidays?"

Jones said quietly, "The North Atlantic Treaty Organization does."

"NATO?" Mike blurted. "Is NATO still in existence? What use is a military alliance in a world where any country, no matter how small, can destroy any other country, no matter how large?"

"I know," Jones said. "When every country on Earth has H-Bombs and intercontinental rockets, they are all equal, militarily speaking, and no combination is any stronger than any individual nation. It's something like the situation in the Old West, when the fellow said, 'All men are created equal. Sam'l Colt made them that way.' Actually, NATO isn't exactly a military alliance any longer. It has—evolved. It's more of an organization on the part of North America and Western Europe to . . . well . . . *control* the Soviet Complex in the realm of international trade."

Mike was scowling at him. "But why the interest in me? I'm just one of hundreds of Horizonal Holidays representatives."

Jones poured the rest of his bottle of beer into his glass. "You are also Michael J. Edwards, the youngest man ever to take the degree of Academician in an American university and you took it in political economy. Three of your textbooks are still in nationwide use."

Mike snorted. "Which didn't keep me from going out on my neck when my department was automated five years ago and TV screens took over teaching."

The other was shaking his head, and there was a certain respect on his Lincolnesque face. "You wouldn't have gone out. A couple of dozen men under you would have been displaced is all. As I understand it, you resigned in protest at their dismissal."

Mike shrugged, somewhat angrily. "I'm not opposed to automation and computers in industry, or anywhere they save drudgery, but I don't believe in it in the arts and certainly not in education. TV has its place but political economy shouldn't be taught to ten million students at once by some joker sitting before a camera. A few decades of that and you'll have everybody in the country with identical ideas."

He thought about it for a moment, before going on. "I suppose I'm in revolt against what's happening to the intellectual in America. With all the manpower available, I think we should put more people into education, science and the arts. I'm not a sulking expatriate. If I came up with an answer to the problems as I see them, I'd return to the States tomorrow and start fighting for the changes I thought necessary to bring her out of the current intellectual and economic rut. Meanwhile, while I'm thinking it out, I'll make my living some other way than in an education system with which I can't agree. Just by chance, this is the job I fell into."

Frank Jones took another swallow of his beer and said, "Professor Edwards—"

"Mr. Edwards, these days."

"All right, Mr. Edwards." Jones seemed to switch subjects. He said, "How would you sum up the world's current economic situation?"

Mike's eyes went around the lobby again. He wondered where Catherina could be. She should be coming in for dinner. Maybe she was off on one of the endless parties the Russkies were forever throwing. He wondered who she was with. That big goof of a Cossack they called Vovo? He wondered if she was sleeping with him. He felt an uncomfortable twang. Jealousy? Holy smokes. He just wasn't the type. And over, of all things, a Russkie tourist.

He brought his attention back to Jones. "Economic situation? Why, looking back it seems unbelievable that we didn't foresee it all. Industrial production, once you get beyond a certain take-off point, can be a geometric progression. You build one steel mill and with its product you build two more, and with their product four more and so on. The Russkies had gotten to that point by 1955 or so and by the 1960s they were fully under way. A planned economy; no depressions, no strikes, no unions to stand in the way of automation. They caught up to American gross national product in the 1970s and kept expanding. Now they're *really* underway and the Chinese and the satellites along with them."

Mike wound it up with, "Is that what you mean?"

Jones flicked a finger at the bartender for another beer. "As far as you go," he said. "I was dwelling on the international aspects."

Mike grunted. "That was our own fool fault. When we refused to trade with them, in the early days, we threw them back on their own resources. By necessity they made themselves self-sufficient. Now the Soviet Complex has no particular need for foreign trade. There's nothing we've got that they require."

"Nothing but one thing," Jones said quietly.

Mike scowled again, not getting it. "What's that one thing?"

"Tourism. The Russians were penned up in their own borders for a couple of generations. Now that travel restrictions have been lifted and prosperity prevails in the

Soviet Complex, tourists are flowing out like water over a broken dam."

Mike shuddered. "You're telling me!" He brought himself back to the original subject. "What in the hell's this got to do with NATO and with me?"

"I'll tell you in a minute," Jones said. "Mr. Edwards, why is there currently a depression in the West?"

Mike said impatiently, "I sound as though I'm giving a course in freshman economics. Actually, we've never recovered from the ending of the cold war. We had a booming economy based considerably on defense production. When a workable peace was arrived at, and the Asian War terminated, that production fell off. In our economy, boom begets boom, but bust also begets bust. Once you start downhill, it's almost impossible to stop. Thus far, we've found nothing to start us booming again."

Jones was nodding, even as he poured himself more beer. "But there's one point you've missed."

Still no signs of Catherina. The other Horizonal Holidays people were filing into the dining room, but there were no signs of Catherina. Confound it. He had several duties later tonight. He'd hoped to be able to have a cocktail or two with the girl.

Mike said, "Look, let's sit down and talk while we eat. I'll have to be going before too long."

They found a table for two and a waiter scurried up with his *lista de platos*. After they had ordered, Mike said, "You were saying something about a point I missed."

"Yes," Jones pursued. "The reason why we've never gotten out of the rut."

"You tell me," Mike said, breaking up a bread roll.

"It's the Russkies. As you pointed out, they're self-sufficient. They don't need international trade. They can consume internally the full production of their industries."

"And?" Mike prompted.

But the waiter was coming up with their food and a bottle of white Metropole wine which Mike had ordered. The dish was *paella*, a favorite of the travel agent, and rich with prawns, fish and small bits of pork in saffron rice.

As they ate, Frank Jones went on. "Our economies of the West are different. Considerably different. Our industries operate only so long as we can sell what they produce. Production is for sale, rather than for use. Under free enterprise we roll along fine when there is a demand for the product. Always in the past we were sparked into new booms by either war, preparation for war, or by foreign trade—by pumping our products overseas, developing new lands, creating new markets abroad."

Mike Edwards took a bite of the Spanish rice dish and nodded. "I wouldn't put it exactly that way, but go on."

"That's it. We can't go on," Jones said dourly. "That's the problem. There are no wars any more, there can't be, or the whole race is doomed. And foreign trade? The Soviet Complex, in spite of the fact that it isn't basically interested in foreign commerce, itself, has for all practical purposes destroyed foreign trade for the rest of the world."

Mike poured them both more of the white wine. He said, "They have indeed. How can we sell typewriters in the Argentine, where they don't manufacture them, when the Russkies come along and dump several shiploads of them into the country to retail for ten dollars apiece?"

The NATO man leaned forward. "That's the point. If the Russkies don't need foreign trade to maintain a healthy economy, why do they bother to raise money by dumping?"

Mike said, "We've already covered that. They don't need our products but they do need foreign exchange for this fabulous tourist outpouring of theirs. Perhaps five million Russkies a year go down to the Argentine, so they need Argentina pesos to pay the tab. The same with every other country to which their tourists go. When you consider some forty million Russkie rubbernecks a year, you realize that they need *lots* of foreign exchange. So they dump. But, once again, what has this got to do with NATO and above all what's it got to do with me."

He let his eyes roam the room again, while waiting for his answer. No Catherina.

Frank Jones nodded his head and looked sour. "To stimulate our economies again, the West has got to get back into international commerce on a large scale. As long as the Soviet Complex is dumping products at cut rates, we can't. And they won't stop as long as they need money for tourism. The answer? The only answer is to figure out some way of stopping the Russian tourists from leaving home."

Mike blinked at him. "Stop them? Holy smokes, how? It's the damnedest phenomenon in the history of travel. They pour over the border of their country like lemmings. And each year it gets worse."

Frank Jones looked down at his glass of wine unhappily. He said, "Beer would go better with this." And then got back to the subject. "Right. And with your background, both academic, and as a working tourist representative handling the Russkies, one of the NATO bigwigs thought you might come up with something."

Mike Edwards leaned back in his chair and laughed. "So that's what you've been building up to for the past hour."

"What's funny?'

Mike said, "My job is that of a tourist representative. Now you want me to figure out some impossible scheme which will drive my best customers—hell, practically my only customers, any more—back to their homeland."

Jones drummed a finger impatiently on the table top. "Good Lord, man, the economies of the whole West are at stake. If you can suggest anything, we need your help desperately."

Mike said, "Well, frankly, I haven't any answer to your problem. In fact, by the looks of things, like I said earlier, it's going to get worse, not better. Production still continues to grow in the Soviet Complex. Next year, Russkie vacations will probably be extended when they make cutbacks in the work week, and the number of months each has to work."

He spotted Catherina and her party coming in the door. Her blonde head was back and she was laughing exuberantly at something that had evidently transpired just before they entered the hotel. Nick Galushko and Ana Chekova were with her, plus Vovo Chervozov who had a guitar and was rendering a Spanish flamenco piece. To render means to tear apart.

Just seeing her tightened Mike's throat. Holy smokes, what had gotten into him?

He came to his feet, deserting the balance of his paella and wine. "Pardon me," he said to Jones. "We'll have to finish this some other time. I'll have to go over and . . . well, sort of check with these people. See if everything is going all right."

Jones looked at the new arrivals. "They look as though

they're going fine. They're already walking two feet off the floor. If you improved things for them, they'd go through the roof."

Mike didn't even hear him. He headed for the table the newcomers had selected.

Nick Galushko was already calling for champagne—four bottles of champagne. Mike inwardly groaned. It was going to be another one of those nights. If he was going to stick around with the group, in order to get next to Catherina, it meant he'd have to go along with them, drink for drink, or damn near it.

VI

In the early morning, nursing a mild hangover, Mike Edwards took his customary one hour, three-mile walk along one of the two Torremolinos beaches. It was the one time of the day he could be quite sure that there would be no demands upon him. None of the Russkie tourists ever arose at dawn. They couldn't, since they invariably caroused until long after midnight and half of them had to be helped to their rooms by hotel servants.

Torremolinos had two beaches, both of fine sand and both sloping gently down into the Mediterranean. The main town beach, known as the Bajondillo, stretched from a rock headland for about two miles in the direction of Malaga. On the other side of the headland, the second beach reached out from in front of the fishing village of Carihuela another mile or so and beyond the last of the tourist hotels, the El Remo. Mike usually alternated his walks, going toward Malaga one day, past Carihuela the next.

He loved the serenity of the Mediterranean with its

gentle tides, its very slight surf. And he loved to watch the fishermen, some of them coming in from fishing all night by arc lamp, some launching their typically Southern Spain-Northern Africa boats, the design of which probably went back to Phoenecian times, for day fishing. Mike Edwards was well known to the fisher folk. When it was out of season and he had time on his hands, he'd often go into their village for a few glasses of wine, or an anis, at the local cantina. It was a part of Spain fast dying in the tourist centers where the bars tended to look the same as tourist bars the world over in their garish decor, their abrasive music, their goddamned loudness.

Now as he progressed he called his Buenos Díases to this acquaintance or that, sometimes waved, sometimes called some jibe at a fisherman who hadn't had much luck the night before. They'd call back, jibe for jibe, sometimes pointing out that at least they made their livings like men —not by herding around mad tourists.

He thought over what Frank Jones had said the night before, and could come up with nothing. In some respects it was even worse than the NATO man had painted it. This flood of Russkies was giving other nations inferiority complexes, lousing up their morale. A few decades before the shoe had been on the other foot. During the Asian War, for instance, Americans spent money in such a way as to rob natives of their feeling of adequacy. An American would get a haircut and misunderstand the barber to say 500 dirhims, rather than 50 dirhims, pay up and then tip them another 50. The barber was robbed of his pride in his trade.

Now the Russians would do much the same thing in the States. They'd buy something, and then say, "How much is that in real money—rubles?" They'd see the Empire State Building and the tour guide would tell them that for a long time, for decades, it was the biggest building in the world. They'd laugh and laugh at that. "That old fashioned monstrosity? Why we have bigger hi-rise buildings than that in small cities such as Kharkov, in the Ukraine; not to speak of Moscow and Leningrad."

Yes, the United States was losing its morale. If something wasn't done soon, it might develop into a permanent disaster.

He made his mile and a half and then turned around and headed back for the path near the rocky headland, which led up to the town proper. He'd return in plenty of time for the breakfast rush of complaints.

A certain amount of submarine life could be observed at the headland, especially with the use of snorkle and mask equipment, but it was now too early for the tourist skin divers. There were half a dozen youngsters, though, scraping the delicious local black mussels from the jagged rocks.

Somewhat to his surprise, at this time of day, he saw what he first assumed to be a fisherman, rod in hand, out on one of the rocks. As he got closer, he realized that it was the Russkie friend of Catherina. What was his name again? Yes. Nicholas Galushko. They called him Nick.

As Mike came up he called to the Russian, "Good morning. They do a little fishing in this area but more ambitious anglers usually prefer to make arrangements with a local boat-owning fisherman to take them out."

Nick Galushko said condescendingly, "Good morning. I'm doing all right."

Mike frowned and said, "Oh, I thought you were fishing."

"I am," the other told him, looking down at what Mike had first thought was an enormous reel.

He stared at him. "But you don't have any line on your . . . rod."

"I don't need any." The Russian pointed to a crevice in the rock upon which he was standing. There were a dozen sizeable fish in it, considerably bigger than the ones even the professional fishermen usually caught in this vicinity. It was not actually good fishing waters and the fishermen almost invariably went much further out and to the south.

Mike looked from the other to the fish and back again.

"Ah ha," the Russian said jubilantly. "A squid. If I catch a squid, will they cook it for me at the hotel?"

"Of course," Mike said blankly. Could the man already be drunk, this time of day? "But, you've broken your line, or something. And how do you know there's a squid out there? They never surface. They stay near the bottom."

There were various studs and buttons on the rod. Nick Galushko flicked a small switch at its tip—if that's what it was—and began to show great signs of agitation.

"Big one," Nick said. "This is the latest fishing equipment from the Black Sea fishing centers. Very latest. Not on the market for sport as yet. I'm testing it in these waters. Very clear water. Better than the Crimea."

He flicked another stud and, shortly, Mike Edwards could make out a large squid coming toward them through the ultra-clear sea. It seemed as though it was being dragged, though dragged by what, Mike certainly couldn't make out. It was at least three times the size of any squid the American had ever seen taken in this vicinity.

When it was close enough, the Russkie reached down, scooped it up by a tenacle and tossed it in with the fish.

He held what looked like a plug in his right hand. It was covered with rather large fishhooks, and looked like a small fish.

"What in the devil is that?" Mike said.

The other laughed boisterously. "I told you. The latest in fishing equipment. Here, I'll show you how it works." He demonstrated what the tourist guide had thought a reel, after tossing the artificial fish back into the sea.

In it was set what would seem to be a small television screen.

"Look in there!" the Russkie commanded.

Mike looked. He seemed to be under the surface of the water. And, actually, he soon realized that he recognized the scene, since he often went skin diving in this vicinity. Yes, the picture being shown was of the area bout thirty feet from the shoreline, and it was getting out further by the minute.

He looked at Nick Galushko, who was beaming with heavy amusement at him. "Where in the name of heaven is that movie coming from?"

"From the eyes in the plug, of course."

"Eyes in the plug!"

"Yes, of course."

"Listen, don't give me that of course routine. There's nothing *of course* about it. You mean to tell me that there's a miniature TV camera in that gadget out there and it's beaming back to the gobblydygook thing you're holding?"

"Of course. Ah, now look. A fish. Ah, too small."

Mike stared again. In the screen they were coming up on what looked to him a fairly good sized red snapper. When they were near enough, the fish seemed to look at them, as though nervously.

"Too small," Nick grunted again. Their camera lens

seemed to point off in another direction and they left the red snapper behind.

Mike shook his head in wonder. "How do you actually catch something, like you did that squid? What happens?"

"The same as other fishing. The fish grabs the bait and you haul it in."

"No line," Mike reminded him.

"You don't need any. Do you see this little stud? You throw it and the plug returns to you, bringing along what you've caught. You catch anything you want."

"What do you mean, you catch anything you want?" Mike said indignantly. Suppose what you want doesn't figure your bait looks very appertizing and says the hell with it?"

"Then I push this switch," the Russian explained, again condescending. "A powerful fish lure is activated. A lure so effective that no fish, at least none that we've run into so far, can resist it."

"Holy smokes," Mike Edwards blurted. "Look, how big a fish can you take with that tackle?" He thought about it. "Could you take a twenty pound salmon?"

"Any size. Well, at least any size that a sports fisherman would likely be interested in. Say, up to five hundred pounds."

"Five hundred pounds! That light tackle?" Mike looked at him as though the other was demented. "Besides, no man alive could wrestle in a five hundred-pound fish, certainly not without the heaviest equipment."

The Russkie demonstrated. "See this little dial? It's for power. If you're fishing for trout or such small fresh water fish, you turn it all the way over here. If you're fishing for, say, a five hundred-pound shark, you turn it all the way around to here. In between, obviously, are for fish in between. Ah, ha. Now here is a better customer. He will go perhaps fifteen pounds, eh?"

Mike said, protest in his voice, "Holy smokes, did you say that you were soon going to put these on the international market?"

"Yes. At thirty dollars a set. We are confident that they will sweep the sport fishing field."

Mike shook his head. "Sweep it? At a price like that, for equipment which will take anything from a trout to a whale, you'll sink the sport fishing field. You'll put every fishing equipment company outside the Soviet Complex out of business overnight."

The Russian yelped, "Got him," and flicked the stud that brought his catch in. He said to Mike, "Well, that would be too bad, I suppose, but business is business, as you capitalists say. Other models are suited to commercial fishing. A great advantage when you can seek out your catch."

Mike Edwards closed his eyes in pain, reopened them again to watch wide-eyed as the other brought in a long, vicious looking fish of a species Mike didn't recognize.

He said, "I'll have to get on up to the hotel. See you later, Mr. Galushko."

He reeled up the path, Frank Jones' words coming back to him again. For the sake of picking up foreign exchange for their tourists, they'd dump this little item on the world market for peanuts, and one more Western field of endeavor would go down the drain.

VII

Two evenings later, Mike Edwards was able to talk a dozen or so of the Russkie vacationists into a tapa tour of Malaga. Actually, he hadn't been stressing the tapa tour this season. He'd had disastrous luck with the Russkies who took it. Something fantastic, something unforeseeable, invariably developed.

The tapa tour consisted of pub-crawling about the multitude of bodegas in Malaga. Tapa means the equivalent of the American free lunch of the pre-World War One days, and the institution still reigned supreme in Spain, although they now sometimes charged a small amount for the tasties. A Spaniard seldom took a drink without something to eat with it: a few shrimp, cheese and bread, french fried fresh sardines, a touch of potato salad, smoked mussels or oysters, a portion of stew. The portions were tiny; so small that you could consume as many as twenty tapas during the course of an evening without killing your appetite for dinner.

Mike's parties would wander up and down the old

streets of the medieval Andulusian city, stopping periodically to have a glass of Sherry here, a small beer there. This had been fine with the British or French tourists, but the Russkies! Ah, the Russkies. They usually started off docile enough, having their *copas* of Sherry or Malaga muscatel, the best in the world, but invariably before the evening was over discipline melted away and the night could end on any note, usually noisy and calamitous, sometimes with several of the tourist group winding up in the local pokey from which Mike would have to bail them out, the following day. The Malaga police took a dimmer view of Russkie tourists than did those of Torremolinos, not being dependent on their spending.

But this was his chance to get Catherina more or less to himself. At least he'd have the opportunity to talk to her. It was difficult in Torremolinos, since she was practically always the center of a group, usually a drunken group dominated by Vovo and his capers. He hadn't invited Vovo to the tapa tour, avoiding the overgrown Cossack.

They drove into Malaga in one of the company buses and started the tour with small glasses of *fino* at Vincente's and the tapa was *gambas pil pil,* a manner of serving small shrimp in a sizzling suace of butter, garlic and red peppers. It is one of the most delicious dishes of Southern Spain. They made enough of a hit with Nick Galushko, Ana Chekova and the others that they had to repeat the performance several times, though the idea of the tapa tour was to take but one tapa at each stop.

Mike didn't mind. It enabled him to get Catherina Saratov off to himself.

They sat at one of the small tables, while the others bellied up to the bar, and Mike came quickly to the point. He said, "Look, why don't you like me?"

Her eyes widened in what would seem to be distress. She said quickly, "But I do. What in the world do you mean, Mr. Edwards?"

Mike said, "Look, call me Mike. You've been avoiding me. At least, unless you're with a group of others. Every time I try to get you alone for a few minutes, you have some excuse."

She sipped at her fino, looked at him over the edge of her glass. She said finally, "Actually, I like you very much Mike. I imagine I always have since, well, since you blushed so hugely there on the beach when you told me about my bathing suit. You have a . . . a boyish quality that I suspect appeals to many women. Certainly it does to me."

He ignored that boyish quality bit, and said, "Well then, why. . . ."

She put a hand on his arm, which didn't make him feel any the worse, but said, "To what end? Do you think that my moral code is looser than that of your Western girls? Admittedly, most of my compatriots are, shall we say, somewhat philosophical about sexual mores, but I assure you, Mike, I'm not." She added mischievously, "In spite of my bathing suit."

Mike flushed. "That's not it at all. I'm sure your code is at least as high as mine. Come to think of it, I suppose mine isn't very high."

She said, "Very well. I leave in a few days. Just what sort of a relationship did you have in mind for us, Mike? A quick—what do you Americans call it?—a roll in the hay? I make no pretentions of virginity, Mike, but I do not go in for—what is the other Americanism?—one night stands."

It struck Mike like a blow. Actually, he hadn't figured it out at length. What did he have in mind? He had never been this attracted to a girl before in his life. But certainly he hadn't had the usual tourist one night stand in mind. He got fed up to here with women who had a quick roll in the hay with their tourist guide in mind. They were a dime a dozen. Hell, they were a nickle a gross in tourist season on the Costa del Sol.

One of the Russkies was roaring questioningly at Mike whether or not they were going to spend the rest of the evening here. He had a tumbler of wine in his beefy hand, rather than the usual small copa glass.

Mike muttered something placating, and took over his guiding duties. He led them down a block or two to the Allegro which was one of the best places in town for draught beer. The Allegro specialized in *callos* for their tapa. They charged slightly for it, but *callos* was well worth it. It was a tripe dish with chick peas and pork fat. You dipped little chunks of bread into the sauce and thanked the Gods for providing such things.

Mike was thinking it over. Catherina was right. What had he in mind? Certainly not a vacation romance, ending for all time when her two weeks were up. Not with Catherina.

While the Russkies were wolfing down their *callos*, with many a shout of approval, he edged her to the side again. "You could stay on," he began feebly.

She laughed at him, albeit sadly. She said, "Mike, Mike. Eventually I'd have to go back to my job, back to Moscow. I work at the Bolshi-Films as a production secretary. I like my work, and I believe that everyone should work. I think you feel the same way, or you wouldn't be here at this type of job, which is below you. I like you. I could probably learn to like you very much more. I know it. But why hurt each other? It simply isn't in our destinies."

Nick Galushko staggered from his place at the bar. He shouted to Catherina to come and try this wonderful new dish. "Do you know what it's made of?" His voice went sly. "I won't tell you until you've tasted."

Catherina laughed. "Tripe, you old glutton. You'd eat anything."

Nick edged her back into the melee, leaving Mike standing alone. He didn't know what he had hoped to accomplish this evening, but whatever it was he wasn't accomplishing it.

The first germ of his idea began to hit him when they were passing the Cathedral on the way to Pepe's where the specialty was Valdepenas white wine with squid deep fried in olive oil for a tapa. It was delicious; one of the best tapas in Malaga, a town noted for its tapas beyond any other save Madrid.

Mike was walking beside Catherina. She said, wonderingly, "Look how the Spanish do when they pass the church. Isn't it fascinating?"

"What?" Mike said.

"They make the sign of the cross. I've read about it. Isn't religion fascinating?"

One of the older Russians, heavyset and now lurching from the evening's wine, said, "When I was a boy my grandmother used to go to church. It was very strange, but, you know . . . she seemed to like it. She had a very strange look on her face when she returned from church each Sunday. You won't believe this, but it was a pleasant, peaceful look. I've always wondered about what they said to her when she went to the church. Very strange."

Catherina turned to Mike Edwards. She said, "Why don't you make the sign of the cross when you pass the

Cathedral? Aren't you religious? I thought that all Westerners were religious."

"Who me?" Mike said. "Oh, sure." He didn't want to disillusion her and, besides, the very beginning of the germ of idea was coming to him. "Only I belong to a different church."

"I didn't know there was more than one," Nick Galushko said. "Is there more than one?"

They were all fascinated. "Religion is a thing of the past in the Soviet Complex," one of them said. "An interesting subject. Tell us about your beliefs. We promise, we won't laugh."

"Of course not," Catherina said indignantly. "It wouldn't be cultured."

Mike thought fast. The tour had hardly begun but already some of them were reeling. They'd probably been soaking it up in Torremolinos, long before he'd had them driven in here to Malaga. He could see what would develop. Somewhere along in here one of them would shout for champagne, or, even worse, vodka, and then the fat would be in the fire. Another of them would begin buying drinks for the house, all the Spanish customers, in one of the bodegas. And before you knew it, Mike would have a brawl on his hands, and eventually cops charging in; the well known Spanish *Guardia Civil* —complete with their hard, medieval hats, complete with billies. Even a few quick bribes might not cool it.

Mike said, "Well, as a matter of fact, what we teach is moderation."

Nick Galushko was charmed by the idea but not quite clear. "Moderation in what?"

"In all things," Mike told him definitely. "In eating, in drink, in smoking. All of the animal pleasures. That's our basic tenet."

Catherina said, "But what has that got to do with religion? Do you know, you're the first really religious person I've ever met."

Mike developed the point. "The idea is that whoever or whatever created you—we're not fanatical about that phase of it—had no intention of you blunting your facilities by overindulgence in any way. Otherwise, why give you keen senses?"

"Why, that's wonderful," Ana Chekova said. "And so obvious."

Mike was doing rather well, he admitted to himself. Especially in view of the fact that he was a life long agnostic. He was a better evangelist than he ever would have thought. He elaborated on the theme, dragging from the depths of memory long neglected words of wisdom from the saints and prophets of yesteryear.

They had arrived at Pepe's where the specialty of the house was the dark, rich, strong Malaga muscatel, some of it as old as seventy-five years. The tapas were varied here, fish soup, cold shrimp, Spanish style potato salad, but none of the Russkies seemed to be in any hurry to sample the wine and food.

Instead, they stood around the table where Mike sat, listening to him expound his gospel, from time to time injecting a word or question. He realized that they were eating it up.

"One of our basic teachings," he said, "is The Golden Rule. Do unto others what you would have them do unto you."

"That's marvelous," Catherina exclaimed. "So obviously and beautifully true."

Mike said, "And another of our basic teachings is that it is better to give than to receive."

That one stopped Nick for a moment. "Why?" he demanded.

Mike explained. "Don't you see? There is more pleasure in sacrificing your own material things for the sake of some one else than there is in being selfish and attempting to acquire more than you possibly need."

"Hmmm," Nick Galushko murmered. "You might be right at that. Tell us more about this religion of yours."

Mike launched into a bit of Zen Buddhism and some of the later Jewish prophets, and then gave them a précis of the Sermon on the Mount, not bothering to give credit to the Author.

Finally he stopped his own sermon and said, "It just occurs to me why you're so fascinated. Religion is taboo in the Soviet Complex, isn't it?"

"Taboo?" somebody said.

"Forbidden," Mike said. "That is, you're not allowed to go to church, to worship."

"Why not?" Catherina was perplexed.

Mike looked at her, perplexed himself. "I don't know. That's what I've always understood."

"Oh," Nick Galushko said. "That was in the old days. Quite a while ago. When the Bolsheviks overthrew the Czar, the churches lined up with the old regime, with the White armies that fought the Red army. So the Bolsheviks had to fight them. It doesn't make any difference any more. I doubt if there's anybody still alive that remembers the Civil War that followed the revolution."

Mike said, "Well then, why hasn't religion returned, if the authorities don't care?"

Nobody seemed to know the answer to that.

"Maybe because there are no longer any churches, except those converted into museums. And there are no longer any priests, or rabbis, or preachers. We read about them in school, but there no longer are any. Not that I've ever heard of, at least," Nick offered. "The whole thing never made much sense to me. That is, of course, until hearing you."

There was a murmer of assent from around the ring at that.

Mike cleared his throat. "Well, we'd better get about having our Malaga muscatel, and then get on to the next place. I can recommend the very old muscatel. It has aged so long that it has become very strong, and very dark and almost as thick as syrup."

They hesitated.

Ana Chekova said sheepishly, "You know, I think I've had enough for tonight. What you've been saying about moderation and all. There's a great deal in that. I've been doing too much drinking. It spoils everything else. I don't even enjoy swimming in the morning. I start off every day with a crashing hangover, and I don't get over it until I've had several more drinks. It's foolishness."

"You're right," one of the other said emphatically.

"Yes," Catherina said, looking from one to the other. "Why don't we get back in the bus and return to Torremolinos?"

They all grunted acceptance of that.

Mike could only stare at them blankly. As a matter of fact he had been anticipating sampling the muscatel himself.

VIII

Mike Edwards was stretched out on his bed, hands behind his head, staring at the ceiling. He had been thinking out the new developments for some time. He had a great deal to think about and the pressures of everyday work weren't conducive to thinking. There were one hell of a lot of ramifications to this.

There was a knock at the door of his small apartment. He kept the place at his own expense, in spite of the fact that he could have had free lodging at any of the hotels that received the flux of his Horizonal Holidays tourists. However, this was a retreat. If he had stayed at a hotel, he knew damn well that the Russkies would be pounding on the door every time he tried to stretch out. The location of this apartment was a secret. But once in awhile somebody would find out about it.

He growled something about tourists and went to answer the summons.

It was Frank Jones, the NATO man.

Mike said, "How in the hell did you know where to find me?"

"I'm a professional," the other said mildly. "Frank Jones sees all, knows all."

Mike said, "It's just as well you turned up. I was thinking about you."

Jones said sourly, "We didn't exactly finish our conversation the other evening, and I haven't been able to find you alone since then."

Mike led the way back to his tiny living-dining-room and motioned to a chair near the table. He went to his sideboard and checked his stock. As usual it was low. Mike Edwards did precious little drinking in his own home. For one thing it was free elsewhere, besides, on an average day he had to put away so much, rather than insult his clients by refusing their hospitality, that he was usually semi-smashed by the time he got back to his place.

There was a half bottle of Fundador cognac. He picked it up along with two small brandy glasses and returned with it to the table. He sat himself down, pulled the cork, poured two drinks and left the bottle open before them.

He said, "This dumping that the Russkies are doing. Do you think that it's a deliberate calculated campaign to undermine the West?"

"No." Jones shook his head. "We've explored that angle, and, no." He took up his glass and sipped the brandy. "You don't have any beer, I suppose?"

"No. Spanish beer is awful and its difficult to get any imports. That's the second best cognac in Spain. Carlos First is the best. Why don't you think it's deliberate? I'm not saying I don't agree with you, but I'd like to know your line of thought."

Jones shrugged, his face in its usual dour expression.

"They're no longer actively trying to propagandize their system. That's an early phase of revolution, when enthusiasms are young and high. Now that they've got luxury on a mass scale, they've become hedonistic. If other countries want to adopt the Russkie socioeconomic system, fine, but let them work it out themselves. They couldn't care less."

Mike thought it over, sipping his brandy. He said, finally, "Well, that covers one important phase of it."

Jones' eyes narrowed. "You think you've got something?"

"Maybe," Mike said. "What do you have in the way of resources to back a program on a large scale?"

"Almost anything, man. Practically unlimited. What's your plan?"

Mike made circles with his cognac glass on the table surface. "We're going to have to give most of the job to Madison Avenue," he mused. "Remember a generation or so ago when the Russkies were first beginning to forge ahead and we were alarmed that their best brains were going into science and production and ours were going into advertising and sales?"

"What in the hell's that got to do with Russkies tourism?" Jones said. He had finished his brandy and now poured another.

Mike said, "We're going to give those bright young men of ours the job of coming up with ideas that will put over the softest sell of all time."

Jones stared at him, as though Mike had suddenly gone around the bend. "Selling what!" he demanded.

"Religion."

Jones couldn't have stared harder if Mike had suddenly sprouted a halo. "Religion!" he blurted. "To whom, and for Christ sakes, why?"

Mike said slowly, "The cold war is a thing of the past, true enough, but the basic battle for men's minds goes on. Frankly, I'm not opposed to the Department of Dirty Tricks when it comes to conflict between ideologies. And both sides use them. Remember back in the Cold War days the story about that shipment of rice that was sent by America to one of the lesser Oriental countries to relieve a famine? Each bag as it was unloaded was weighed by a native official while another native stenciled something on the bag. American Embassy officials were standing by but, because they had never bothered to learn the native language, they didn't realize that the native stenciling the bags was lettering them: *This Rice is a Gift From the Soviet Union.*"

Jones laughed sourly. "I'd forgotten about that one. If we were too foolish to learn the native language, we deserved to be gypped. But what's the 'dirty trick' you're obviously building up to?"

Mike said, "Well, dirty trick isn't the word exactly. But for half a century and more the Russkies haven't been exposed to religion, in spite of the fact that the Slavs are traditionally one of the most religious races on Earth. Remember, they called it Holy Russia in the Czar's day? Well, for the first few decades of the commies they fought religion tooth and nail, taught atheism in the schools, closed up the churches, gave the priests and other religious teachers a hard time. Very well. The old generation slowly died off and the new one was without religion, and the next generation following. The government doesn't care now. It's no longer an issue that threatens the State."

Jones was obviously disappointed. He knocked back the remainder of his cognac before saying, "I don't see any connection with our need to cut off the Russkie flow of tourists."

Mike ignored him. "We'll have to plan it carefully, very hush-hush. We'll send our boys into the country, spreading religion; the Russkies will be inordinately receptive."

"Why will they?" Jones scowled. "And who the hell gives a damn?"

Mike waggled a finger at him. "People are prone to new religions at two periods. First, in the beginning of their society when luxuries are almost unknown, life hard and the simple virtues a necessity. Look at we Americans when we were settling the West, the hard way. Were straight-laced, hard working, church-going, tight mouthed—let's face it, fanatics. You couldn't have found one atheist or agnostic in a hundred of them. The second period when a people are particularly prone to the lure of religion is during their decadence. Through pure boredom they seek out new experiences, new ways of achieving excitement. Rome is an example. In their first centuries they had a conservative religion and they were devout, but in their final centuries the old straight-laced religion disappeared and many exotic new ones swept in from Egypt and the Orient."

Jones still didn't get it. He poured himself another slug of the brandy, all but belligerently. He said, "But what's the point? What kind of new religion? What will these missionaries teach?"

"The Old Time Religion, of course. The virtues of the simple life. The glories of the home. Puritanism. Once it got under way, we'd lay heavy stress against ostentatious display of wealth such as in foreign travel. Stay at home and cultivate the simple virtues, that's the pitch."

Jones was shaking his head. "It wouldn't work. It

might for awhile, as a fad; they're great for fads, but then something else would come along. Some other fad."

Mike pressed his point. "That's all we need. A couple of years. Stop the tourist trade for only two or three years and the Russkies would stop dumping their products on the world market. They wouldn't need the foreign exchange. That would revive commerce between the Western countries. A new boom would start. Once under way, boom begets boom. New factories, at least as automated and computerized as the Russkies, would go up. By the time the Russkies had become interested in tourism again, we'd be under full sail."

Mike shrugged. "What'll happen then, I don't know. We can face that problem when it arrives."

Jones was shaking his head again. "The NATO council would never accept it. You can't toy with something as vital as religion."

Mike was contemptuous of that opinion. "Don't be ridiculous, Frank. I'm not suggesting that we teach them voodooism. This isn't the first time plain. ordinary religion has been used as an economic lever. And how can the Russkies lose? When it's all over, it will only mean that religion has been reintroduced into the Soviet Complex. Those Russkies that like it will adopt it permanently, those that don't, won't. Nobody's twisting anybody's arm. Once the movement starts, undoubtedly other religions will be re-established, Judaism, Mohammedism, the various branches of Christianity."

Jones slapped the table with the palm of his hand. "I think it's worth a try, at least. We can put it before the higher-ups."

Mike said, "Yeah. And if they accept and it works, I'll be looking for another job. Come to think of it, possibly as an evangelist in Moscow. Besides spreading the gospel to our friends, the benighted Russkies, I have in mind some personal business to attend to there."

He looked at his watch. "I've got to get going now. Tomorrow, one of my groups terminates its vacation and returns north. We hold a masquerade for them at La Manana nightclub tonight. I've got to get into my matador costume. I've worn it to so many of these masquerades that it's beginning to need patching." He brightened. "Maybe the holes in it will look like places I've been gored.

"It couldn't happen to a nicer guy," Jones said, beginning to feel scepticism about Mike's idea, all over again.

Actually, it was Catherina's last evening and Mike couldn't allow himself to miss it. Especially since the rumor was that she was to appear in the costume of a Cretan Goddess of the Minoan period. Mike Edwards would no more have missed witnessing Catherina Saratov as a Cretan Goddess than he would have, well, than he would have anything . . .

IX

As a Cretan Goddess of the Minoan period, Catherina Saratov turned out to be a wow. Mike Edwards' duty called upon him to protest her decolletage, in view of Spanish mores. Decolletage wasn't quite the word for it. Some more extreme terminology was called for. It seemed as though Cretan women of the Minoan period went topless, or so nearly so that it made no difference. Evidently, they were vain of their bosoms and didn't mind showing them.

And evidently Catherina Saratov was also proud of her bosom and didn't mind displaying it. As a matter of fact, not a man present protested, neither Spaniard, Russkie nor the sole representative of America—Mike Edwards.

Mike was nothing if not masculine. He didn't have it in him to suggest that she at least utilize a little gauze in concession to Spanish codes of modesty.

Well, there were precious few Spaniards around, if any, besides the bartenders and waiters. The Russkies had taken over the establishment en masse.

Ordinarily, at one of these masquerades, Mike Edwards let the guests go to hell in their own way, but this time there was a Machiavellian quality in his arrangements. He put place cards on the tables; not that most of them paid much attention, prefering to seek out the friends they'd made during their Spanish weeks. His place card, obviously, was at the same table with her two friends, Nick Galushko and Ana Chekova. Vovo Chernozov was seated at the far end of the nightclub—as far away as possible. Vovo didn't seem to mind. He was already feeling no pain. But then, Mike had never seen the two-ton Cossack in a state of less than complete intoxication. The other was costumed, now, as the Siberian plainsman he was, and looked somewhat like Tamerlane or Ghengis Khan, complete to a bull whip, which he was having a time flourishing off and on.

Ana Chekova, with a great lack of taste, was attired as a ballet dancer, which made not only Mike Edwards wince, but everyone else in the room. Nick Galushko was done up as a capitalist. Or at least what the Russkies thought a capitalist ought to look like. He had a formal silk hat on, and formal morning suit. Mike wondered where in the hell he could have got the outfit.

Catherina Saratov beamed in friendly smiles as Mike took his chair next to her. She said, "How nice it turned out that you were to be seated with us. But it is on my conscience. We have taken up so much of your time this past few weeks that I am afraid you have neglected the others."

Mike made every effort in the world to keep his eyes from her pink tipped breasts. Holy smokes, the Cretan man must have been driven frantic.

He cleared his throat and looked out over the room of laughing, shouting, roaring Russkies. He said, "They don't seem to be neglected. Our original plans for these parties were to serve free *sangria,* but nobody seems to go in for Spanish wine punch."

"For babes," Nick Galushko snorted overbearingly. He waved at a waiter. "Another bottle of vodka and two magnums of your horrible champagne. Tonight we must celebrate a return to the Soviet Complex and *real* Armenian champagne, sweeter and with twice as much alcohol."

Mike Edwards shuddered. It was going to be a long night. He could see that it was going to be one of those nights. If, after a couple of more years of this life, he still had a liver he'd be lucky.

He said, "A little later the band will come in and it will be possible to dance."

"Oh, how wonderful," Cathernia said, honoring him with a smile that produced certain sexual reactions in him that he couldn't possibly have fulfilled here and now. "Do you dance . . . Mike?"

He was glad she had gotten over the Mr. Edwards bit. He was about to tell her that if he didn't dance, he would have learned tonight. He wasn't going to miss the chance of holding those two things of her's up against his chest, if it was the second to the last thing he ever did. The last being to kick off.

"Yes," he said. "I did quite a bit when I was a teenager and when I was in college."

"You'll have to teach me some of the new American steps," she told him. "The Americans are always in the forefront when it comes to new dancing. What a wonderful opportunity. I refuse to dance with anyone but you this whole evening. I understand that in the newest dance step from Ultra-New York that both sit on the floor. It seems a very strange manner in which to dance, but I would like to try."

All of which was okay with Mike Edwards, except that he had no intention of sitting on the floor. He had every intention of letting her know that the very *latest* of steps from that font of new steps, America, involved holding the girl—very closely.

Nick Galushko had a sizeable camera in hand and was merrily banging away in all directions, though the room was as dim as gloom, taking this last opportunity to get snapshots of friends made on this vacation.

Mike said, trying to make his voice such that it wouldn't set the other off, "I . . . I'm afraid there's not enough light in here, Nick, for pictures without flash."

Nick grunted his contempt of that opinion. "This camera doesn't need flash," he said condescendingly. "It's the new model Mikoyan. It doesn't need light. It supplies its own light. Not the kind we use. I'm not up on the technical angles, but you could take a picture of a bullet in flight, in a pitch dark room. It also takes either 3-D or ordinary pictures. Has immediate development and either color or black and white, of course."

Mike stared at him. "No light?"

The Russkie nodded. "That's right, no light. It's coming out in the Fall. We're going to sell them for ten dollars apiece."

Nick Galushko pulled a picture from the back of the camera and held it over to Mike Edwards. He said, "Immediate development."

Mike looked at it. It was beautifully done. A shot of Vovo, the Cossack, which captured him perfectly. The big man was perfectly centered, champagne bottle in hand, the background faded a bit so that only he stood out. It could have been submitted most successfully to any photography contest.

The American had to say, "You're quite a photographer, Nick. This is beautifully composed and you haven't even had it in a dark room to be touched up."

"In the first place, you don't need to work in a dark room with a Mikoyan photo," Nick told him. "If there's any touching up you want to do, you can do it in ordinary light. Enlarging, all that sort of thing. But it's seldom there's any cause to. However, I'm no photographer. I don't have to be. With this camera all you have to do is point it at the subject and press the trigger. Everything else is taken care of."

Mike said, "Well, I was talking about the composition and so forth."

"The composition is taken care of too. A child can operate this."

Mike stared at him, uncomprehending.

The Russian said condescendingly, "The West is way behind in photography. When you press the trigger—is that what you call it?—the lens checks back to the computer banks in Leningrad——"

"Computer banks," Mike said weakly.

". . . and they size up the situation and swivel the lens about for the best composition possible, adjust the shutter and light—the camera's light, not the kind we know—and flick the shutter when the subject is in an interesting pose. The tight beam back to Leningrad is instantaneous, of course, and so are the computers, so everything happens immediately."

Mike closed his eyes in anguish.

Nick laughed. "Where the real profit will come in is when the camera owners have to buy all their film from us. We're the only source of this new light emulsion arrangement. Oh, we'll clean up."

Inwardly, Mike Edwards groaned again. There went the photo industry of the West. The United States with its Kodaks, and Polaroids, Germany with its Leicas, Japan with its Nikons. All down the drain. No photographer in his right mind would do without one of these practically free Mikoyans. Not only that but every professional photographer would overnight become unemployed. Who'd be silly enough to hire a professional, when the computer banks in Leningrad guaranteed a perfect shot?

Galushko, with his maddening condescension, was saying, "It all goes back a generation or so. When you Americans, and the others, were allowing their best brains to go into advertising, entertainment and sales, and whatever, we were devoting our best brains to science, engineering and technology. When your young people had Bing Crosby and Rita Hayworth as their pinups, or some football hero, we had scientists for ours. Now we reap the results."

It was practically the same thing Mike had said to Jones earlier in the evening, which didn't make it any easier to take.

"Holy smokes," Mike said, meaninglessly.

The waiter came up with the three bottles Nick had ordered, three champagne glasses and three large shot glasses for the vodka, on a tray. But before he could put it down on the table, the Russian had grabbed up one of the bottles of bubbly wine and was working away at the cork. He let fly with it at some friends at a nearby table and they yelled laughter. Two of them grabbed up champagne bottles in turn, and popped the corks back.

Within moments, the whole nightclub was at it, the Russkies calling demandingly at the suffering waiters for more bottles of champagne.

At this rate, Miek Edwards decided, La Manana would be completely out of champagne within a half hour. Not that Pepe, the manager, would mind. However, the cleanup women in the morning undoubtedly would. Half of the wine was foaming out of the bottles onto the floor. But there was enough remaining that if the revelers drank it all—and he'd never seen a Russkie yet who left a part emptied bottle—there wouldn't be a one able to get back to his hotel on his own feet.

The battle was ended by the arrival of the orchestra, which began to set up on the dias provided for musicians at the far end of the bar. Mike realized, unhappily, that he'd made a mistake in placing Vovo Chernozov in that vicinity. Already the big Cossack was eyeing the drums with happy interest. Mike would have bet a dollar to a subway slug that before the evening was out, Vovo would be up there, ignoring the protests of the professional drummer and pounding away at the skins.

Ana Chekova entered the conversation for the first time since Mike had come in. She said to him, "You Americans have a very strange sense of humor."

He said reasonably, "Well, I suppose that every nationality has its own type of humor. I've never been able to understand the British, for instance."

She wasn't having any of that. She downed her glass of champagne and said, "I heard a joke today, told by one American to two others. And they laughed and laughed. But it made no sense at all."

Mike said, "Well, do you remember it? Perhaps I could explain. Possibly translate it into Russian for you. It's sometimes difficult to understand humor in a language other than your own."

She looked at him coldly. "I teached advanced English in Kiev. I remember the story very well. I have an excellent memory."

"All right," Mike said agreeably. "Let's hear it."

Ana launched into the joke. "Cinderella wanted to go to a ball and her fairy godmother—"

"What's a fairy godmother?" Catherina said to Mike.

"Something like an elf. Supposedly, when each child is born, it is given a fairy godmother who watches over it all its life."

Ana ignored the interruption and went on. "Her fairy godmother said that, all right, she could go to the ball but she would have to return home by midnight, or her pussy would turn into a pumpkin."

Mike Edwards winced, realizing what kind of joke must be coming up.

She went on. "So Cinderella went to the ball and her fairy godmother waited up for her, ominously. Midnight came but there was no Cinderella. So the fairy godmother picked up the telephone and called the place where the ball was being held and demanded to talk to Cinderella. When Cinderella came to the phone the fairy godmother said, 'You know what I told you, don't you? If you didn't return by midnight, your pussy would turn into a pumpkin.' And Cinderella said, "Yes, I remember.' And the fairy godmother said, in surprise, 'Well, what happened? Why aren't you home?' And Cinderella said, 'Oh, I met the most wonderful man.' And the fairy godmother said, "Man! What's his name?' And Cinderella said, 'His name is Peter, Peter . . . something or other."

Nick poured more champagne and a slug of vodka for each of them. "Is that all?" It doesn't sound very funny to me, either."

Once again, Mike's eyes were closed wearily.

Catherina had two faint lines above her eyes. She said to Mike, "What's a pussy?"

He cleared his throat and said, "American idiom for

a small cat." The orchestra had begun to play. He said, "Would you like to dance?"

"Oh, yes, of course." She was on her feet immediately, her breasts jiggling prettily at the motion.

Mike had noticed in the past that Russkies didn't usually shine at ballroom dancing, no matter what their reputation in ballet. Oh, they were enthusiastic enough, especially after a few drinks, and expended endless energy, but the Slavs evidently didn't have the flare for it that the young people of the West did. He followed Catherina out onto the dance floor, the first couple to arrive, and took her into his arms.

She leaned back slightly, in surprise. "I thought that in most modern dances the partners didn't touch each other."

He took her more firmly to him. "That's old hat," he said. "The latest thing is the Two-Step. The man holds the girl right up against him, his right arm around her waist, their left hands joined like this. You'll catch on in no time at all. Later, I'll demonstrate the waltz."

"Waltz?" she said in surprise. "But we do that in the Soviet Complex. It's one of the oldest dances of all, isn't it?"

"It's going through a great revival," Mike told her. "Later, I'll get the musicians to play some waltzes and we'll practice."

She snuggled closer to him. "I'll leave it to you. It would be uncultured not to take the advice of an expert."

Actually, she turned out to be a moderately good dancer, he found. His own comparative skill was such that they made themselves the stars of the dance floor. His colorful *trajes de luces,* his matador's suit of lights, combined with her spectacular Cretean costume, didn't detract from the show.

The Russkies entered into the spirit of the dance with a vim. Which wasn't surprising to Mike. Most of them were already smashed and the champagne and vodka were still going down like water. He closed his mind to the tragedies that probably lay ahead, before the evening was through, and devoted himself to his dream world.

They danced the first three dances together before Vovo got around to reeling over to their table and requesting Catherina for the next one. She laughingly declined on the grounds that she was thirsty. Vovo reeled off again, seeking an alternative victim.

Catherina laughed and said, "I can just feel that overgrown oaf walking all over my slippers. Besides, I promised every dance to you tonight, Mike."

"I'm not arguing," he said.

However, the next time they got onto the dance floor, Mike could see the scowl on Vovo's face. That wasn't so good. Thus far, the Cossack had been a genial drunk. But there was no good reason to believe that he couldn't be a mean one, given what he thought was provocation.

When the dance was over and they'd returned to their table again, where Nick and Ana had gotten down to some really serious drinking, Vovo came reeling over once more, his peasant face dour.

He said to Catherina, "This next dance must be mine. I have ordered the band to play a Cossack polka."

Catherina said, "Oh, please, Vovo, not me. I don't know how to dance the polka."

"Very well. I will teach you." The hulk of a man looked at Mike Edwards. "This fancy pip isn't the only one who can teach dancing."

She said, "Please, Vovo. I don't want to dance this one."

"Then the next!"

Mike Edwards said gently, "Mr. Chernozov, Miss Saratov obviously doesn't want to dance with you. Perhaps she thinks you've had a bit too much wine."

"Da, go on away, Vovo," Nick Galushko slurred. "You'd break her leg."

The Cossack ignored that opinion and swayed a bit as he eyed Mike balefully. He said finally, "Well, if Catherina won't perform with me on the floor, how about you? I challenge you to wrestle with me, Turkoman style!"

X

Silence dropped momentarily.

Then Ana Chekova, her face red with drink, muttered woozily, "Oh, don't be a fool, Vovo."

Vovo said with drunken formal dignity. "If he wishes to take my woman, then he must be ready to fight for her —Turkoman style."

"I'm not your woman," Catherina flared up. "I am no one's woman."

He leered at her. "We'll see about that."

She shot a quick, embarrassed look at Mike Edwards.

All right, Mike told himself. Put up or shut up. You can't back down in front of the woman you're pursuing. He sighed, inwardly, and stood. If he won, he'd probably get fired for beating up a customer of Horizonal Holidays. If he lost, he'd probably have a few broken bones and a face that looked like hash.

He said, "I can't fight you Turkoman style, simply because I don't even know what Turkoman style is. But I'll fight you my own way, and you can fight any way you wish."

The big Cossack stared at him, unbelievingly. Without a doubt he had expected victory by default. He snorted deprecation and turned and shouted in Russian, "Clear the floor!"

Catherina, in alarm, put a hand on Mike's arm. "Mike," she said. "Don't be insane. He is champion of his Soviet Republic. I believe I know what you are thinking, but it is ridiculous. I'll understand, if you back down."

Nick was staring at him, seemingly somewhat more sober. "Don't be crazy," he said. "Did you see what he did to that bull in Malaga?"

Mike had seen, all right, all right. And one thing was obvious. Vovo was able to operate whilst up to his eyeballs in alcohol. Happily, Mike himself had been too preoccupied with Catherina and the dance to have done much drinking himself, because he couldn't operate even partially when stoned.

He shucked out of his matador's jacket since it was too stiff with gold and other lace for proper movement. But Vovo didn't bother. Evidently, his Cossack dress lent itself to rough and tumble.

The dance floor had cleared magically. Inwardly, Mike Edwards groaned. The floor, of course, was wooden, no sort of mat on which to work, not even a rug. It was going to be brutal.

Vovo had marched out onto the floor. Now he turned and faced his opponent, going into a wrestler's crouch.

It had been years since Mike Edwards had been on the student and faculty team. He had kept himself in reasonable shape, but he was rusty, rusty as all get out, and Vovo was not only a champ but evidently *currently* champ.

He threw himself into the *Hackiji-dachi,* spreadout position, with his left foot slightly forward and his body weight evenly distributed and in a well-balanced pose. Both fists were clenched, knuckles facing down and held slightly to the side of his waist, with his toes pointed slightly inward.

In actuality, his clothing wasn't bad for karate fighting. Matadors had to be able to move lithely, and his bull fighting slippers lent themselves to the game he was attempting to play.

Vovo was, on the face of it, taken aback by the stance Mike had assumed. Obviously, it meant something. And inwardly, Mike thanked whatever gods there might be, if any, that the other had probably never seen Japanese hand-to-hand fighting in his life. It was Mike's only chance.

Vovo, now in action, was seemingly completely sober. It was astonishing how the man could throw off the effects of alcohol. He came in, arms spread, knees slightly bent, and then suddenly rushed.

Mike used the Backward Mule Kick. As Vovo came in, he stepped back on his left foot and after completely turning his body around, dropped with both hands to the floor. With his right leg, he kicked the Cossack in the stomach as hard as he could, refraining from slamming the man in the groin instead, the original idea of this particular kata.

Vovo's stomach was like iron, in spite of all his high living, but he was thrown backward. The rest of the Russkies laughed uproariously at his discomfort. They had no doubts, of course, about the final conclusion but it was amusing to see their champion given a temporary setback in this bout with the comparatively puny American tourist manager.

Vovo came semi-erect again and glared thoughtfully at the smaller man. He had truly expected the whole thing to be over in a matter of moments. But, once again, Vovo was no fool in hand-to-hand combat. He had not become champion of the Soviet Republic of his birth by being a fool. This time he moved in more carefully; he was fighting in a field utterly unknown to him.

And inwardly, Mike Edwards cursed. He had hoped that the other, full of alcohol, and full in the eyes of is compatriots, would go berserk and charge heedlessly. But, it could be seen, Vovo did not underestimate a foe, no matter how much smaller the foe. Mike had few illusions; if the powerful Russkie ever got his hands on him, he was sunk. The man was a giant and except for that ring of lard about the back of his neck, there wasn't an ounce of fat on him.

Mike fell into the *Kokutsu-dachi,* layout position, his right foot forward with toes pointing straight forward and knees slightly bent, carrying about 30 percent of his body weight. The left leg carried about seventy percent. The rear leg knee was bent as much as possible, with the toes pointed outward and forward. It was his favorite defensive karate position.

The Cossack wrestling champion came in quick this time. He knew good and well that if he could get his hands on Mike, get him down on the floor, it would all be over in a matter of moments.

Mike's mind was spinning. The other moved much too fast for a man of his size. And he was obviously cool in combat. Mike was going to have to come up with something really devastating. In the long run, if he allowed it to become a long run, the other would have him.

He decided on the Ninth Kata, when Vovo threw a right punch. He grabbed the Cossack's wrist with his left hand, walked around and grabbed the other's right shoulder with his right hand, slamming Vovo's chin with an elbow punch. Simultaneously, he moved in quickly with his right foot to come around to the Russian's right side rear legs. With his own right foot he kicked forward and then quickly backwards against the other's rear leg, knocking him to the floor. He didn't release the other's right hand wrist as he hit the flooring but held him and gave him a right foot heel stamp across the solar plexus as he held him to the floor.

He came down quickly and with his right hand chopped down to the Russkie's adams apple, once again holding the punch. It was possible to kill, at this point.

Vovo was attempting to roll out and Mike had to exert his full strength.

Still holding his hand wrist lock, he knelt down on the floor on his left knee on the right side of his opponent. With his right knee raised off the floor, he brought his left hand wrist lock that he was still holding and lay it across the top of his right knee. He was now in a position to push the left hand wrist lock downward and with his right hand pull up the upper arm, thus breaking Vovo's arm.

He couldn't do it.

And then something hit him. What, he never found out.

When he regained consciousness, it was to find himself on the floor, his head in Vovo's lap, the emotional Cossack crying.

Several score others seemed to be packed around. Somewhere he could hear Nick Galushko yelling angrily. And then Mike got it. His tablemate was yelling for a doctor.

Mike shook his head blearily. He still didn't know

what had happened. He sucked in air and said up into the Cossack's face, "You won."

The other shook his head, still tearfully. "I am no fool. Twice you could have finished me. Very seriously finished me. And you are a smaller man. You should have finished me when you had the chance."

For the first time, Mike noticed that Catherina, her breasts complete free of her bodice, was on her knees on the other side of him.

Mike said, "Let me up. Holy smokes, I'll probably get sacked by my company for this display." He staggered to his feet, still wobbly. What in the hell had the damn Russian hit him with, a table?

Vovo said, with uncharacteristic, sober decisiveness, "Not if the signature of every member of this vacation tour means anything."

Catherina said, "Come over here and sit down."

"I'm all right," Mike said, in self disgust.

But they led him to the table. The other Russkies dropped away to their own places. On the way to the table, supporting Mike with one arm, Vovo snagged another bottle of champagne from a friend's table. He got Mike back into his chair, pulled up another one and sat himself down, looking anxiously at the tourist guide.

As Catherina, Ana and Nick took their own seats, Vovo said, "How do you feel? It was a nasty trick that I pulled, eh? But I was desperate, Mike. You had me in a very bad spot."

"In that kind of fighting," Mike said woozily, "there is no such thing as nasty tricks. It's all based on nasty tricks. The idea is to win, whatever way. You won, fair and square."

Vovo took up the champagne and began to pour for

them all. "Here," he said. "Perhaps this will make you feel better."

But, surprisingly, Nick Galushko shook his head and put a palm over the top of the glass. "Not for me," he said. "I've had enough. I have had more than enough."

They all looked at him, including Mike, who was feeling better by the minute. Nick seemed to be sober. Twenty minutes ago he'd been potted.

He looked at Mike and said, "While you two were making fools of yourselves out there on the floor, what you told us the other night came back to me."

Vovo hadn't been on the tapa tour. He looked from Nick to the American and back again. "Ha, Comrade Galushko, what did he tell you that would make a bottle man such as yourself refuse a drink?"

Nick said definitely, "That we should practice moderation in all things. If everyone had been less drunk, there would have been no fight between two grown men over a woman that belongs to neither, and, I assume, has no desire to belong to either."

Ana Chekova thought about it and said, "Nick's right. Instead of having a truly good time tonight, practicing moderation, we all get stupid drunk, most of us well on the way to passing out. And in the morning we will have terrible hangovers to fly back with us to the Soviet Complex. How stupid of us."

Vovo thought about it too. He looked at Mike. "Where did you get this idea?"

Here we go again, Mike thought inwardly. However, it was a good chance to feel out the program he had suggested to Frank Jones.

He said, "It's the teaching of the Old Time Religion Church, to which I belong." He might have added, *being the founder and charter member. In fact, thus far being the only member.*

"Church?" the big Cossack said blankly.

"That is correct," Mike said with considerable dignity. "As far back as 500 B.C. Theognis, the Greek poet and philosopher taught, 'Be not too zealous; moderation is best in all things.' Ever since, wise men have stressed the same teaching."

"Who, besides this Greek?" Vovo demanded, scowling as he considered the idea.

Mike Edwards was on fairly firm ground. Earlier that day, before talking with Jones, Mike had gone to the home of a British friend, who had a fairly extensive library, and borrowed his Bartlett's *Familiar Quotations,* and had checked out MODERATION.

He said, "Euripides, the Athenian tragic poet, circa 484-406 B.C., put it this way: 'Moderation, the noblest gift of heaven.'"

He pretended to consult his memory. "More recently, Joseph Hall, Bishop of Norwich in the 17th Century, said, 'Moderation is the silken string running through the pearl chain of all virtues.'"

"Why, how beautifully stated," Catherina said, admiration in her eyes. The admiration was obviously for Mike rather than the good bishop.

Other Russkies, at nearby tables, were listening in, especially those who had been on the tapa crawl. Several of them came to their feet and crossed over to the table where the conversation was going on.

One of them whispered to several of the others, sotto voce, "It's what I was telling you about. Religion. Fascinating, eh?"

Vovo said, only half arguing, "Who can you point out that ever profited by this moderation teaching? Who ir history ever got anywhere practicing moderation? Some say you must live to the hilt. Eat, drink and be merry, for tomorrow we die." He looked about him, frowning. "Where does that quotation come from?"

Mike knew damn well where it came from. It came from the Bible and was in both *Ecclesiastes* and *Luke*. But he wasn't about to say so.

He said, instead, "Who in history ever got anywhere who didn't practice moderation? What artist can work if he befuddles himself with too much drink? What scientist can come up with great discoveries, if he is a victim of, say, narcotics? What great statesman can control the destinies of his country if he spends most of his time chasing women? Who could be a great soldier if he was overly fat, from eating too much?"

"Napoleon," somebody said.

Oh, oh. He flunked that time. How could he cover? It came to him. He shook his head definitely. "When Napoleon first began making his great victories, he was thin. Later, both when he invaded Russian, and at Waterloo, he was so fat that he spent too much time in his bed. After he became obese, the defeats started."

"Alexander the Great was one of the best generals of all time, and a heavy drinker," someone said, argumentively.

"And he drank himself to death in his early thirties," Mike countered.

"Well put," Nick Galushko said.

The Russians, practically all of them in the nightclub, were packed around the table now.

Ana Chekova said, "What else do you teach in this Old Time Religion Church of yours?"

Mike thought quickly. He wanted to put over more of

the anti-living-it-up bit. He said, "We consider these to be our basic principles:

"Blessed are the poor in spirit; for theirs in the kingdom of heaven.

"Blessed are the meek: for they shall inherit the earth.

"Blessed are they which do hunger and thirst after righteousness: for they shall be fulfilled.

"Blessed are the merciful: for they shall obtain mercy.

"Blessed are the pure in heart: for they shall see God."

"*Zut!*" Catherina exclaimed. "How beautiful. Who wrote that?"

Mike cleeared his throat. "A very good man, a couple of thousand years ago." He realized, somewhat to his astonishment, that he had them all in the palm of his hand.

Pepe, the Le Manana manager, was glaring at him from the bar. All drinking had stopped.

XI

Mike Edwards walked Catherina Saratov back to the Hotel Triton which was located on the Montemar beach, just beyond Carihuela. It was one of the swankier establishments in Torremolinos. The Russkies invariably took over all the deluxe and first class hotels, leaving what remained for more proletarian nationalities. It wasn't necessarily a matter of any individual Russian tourist being wealthier than, say, a Frenchman or German, it was just that the Soviet Complex government picked up all vacation tabs for all Russians, and rented, in blocks, out from under everybody else. Expense was of no moment.

La Manana was located on the square, the plaza in the center of Torremolinos proper. The resort town had by now spilled out for a mile or so in all directions, but the square and a couple of blocks about it were all that remained of the old fishing village and art colony of Torremolinos.

Mike could have taken a cab, but he welcomed the opportunity to continue Catherina's company, especially alone. The other Russkies had all preferred transportation.

They walked slowly, out the main highway to Gibraltar, about a hundred miles to the south, and at first had little to say. He wondered if she'd mind if he took her hand, but decided against it.

So finally she took his.

After a time, when they had arrived at the outskirts of that part of town devoted to shops, restaurants and nightclubs and were beginning to get to the long row of tourist hotels, Catherina said, and there was a frown in her voice, though he couldn't see her face in the dim of the night, "Mike, this Old Time Religion Church to which you belong. Are you quite . . . well, devout?"

"Oh, yes." What could he say after that lengthy sermon he had just given?

She said, "And you believe all this about moderation in all things?"

"Yes, of course."

"But you drink. And there you were willing to fight in public. And you go to such spectacles as bullfights. How do you reconcile all this with leading a life of moderation?"

Oh, oh. He was going to have to think fast.

He said, "Well, yes. I can see your point. And I agree with it. For a time I tried to tell myself that it was necessary to do these things for the sake of my job. But now, after considerable meditation, I realize that this is insufficient excuse. So what I've decided to do is go home and take Holy Orders."

"Holy Orders?"

"Yes. I am going to become a minister of the gospel," Mike said piously.

"You *are*? Oh, how wonderful," Catherina said. "You'll be working then for what you really believe in."

"That's right." In a way he was hating himself for . . . well, it wasn't quite lying to her, because he actually was going to found the Old Time Religion Church. However, the reason was another thing.

They were approaching her hotel, and lapsed into silence again. He took her arm as they marched across the hotel lobby, and groaned inwardly. The night had been too warm to call for a wrap. The Cretean costume was all Catherina wore. And she wore it proudly; her full breasts on proud display. Topless bathing suits were prevalent in the States, and he knew that the same applied to the Soviet Complex. In fact, completely nude bathing was far from unknown on the Soviet beaches. But somehow, as he watched from the sides of his eyes, in spite of himself, the mammary glands of the woman he loved, he agonized, shouldn't be on display for others.

The Hotel Triton was not so plebian as to have rooms, but only suites. All faced the sea; all had terraces. All were lavishly furnished and decorated in the finest of Spanish lack of taste. How they managed it, Mike had never figured out, but Spanish architecture, Spanish decor, contemporary Spanish paintings, were the most sterile in the world. Hell, they were grim.

Mike had expected to be dismissed at the door, sweetly, kindly, but dismissed. He had not even aspired to a gentle peck of a kiss on his cheek from the woman he yearned for like a goddamned high school teenager after his first piece of ass. How he had ever gotten to this point, he told himself for the tenth time, he'd never know. The potential sex-life of a tourist guide on the Costa del Sol, in season, would have put a Don Juan or Casanova to shame. Potentially, he had a harem that a

Turkish sultan would have envied. Usually, that very fact all but drove him to impotence.

But he wasn't dismissed.

Catherina said, "Won't you come in for a last nightcap? Isn't that what you Yankees call it, a nightcap?"

"Yes," Mike said, thankful for the invitation. It would give him another ten minutes or so with her. And she was due to leave in the morning. But then, duty bound, he said, "I'm not a Yankee, you know."

She was leading him into the living room of her small suite. The faint lines above her eyes, that he loved, the tiny frown, manifested themselves. "No? But I thought you told me you were."

"I'm from New Mexico, in the western part of the United States, and my people before me were from Florida, in the south. Southerners don't like to be called Yankees. Yankees are from New England, in the northeast. It's as though you called a Bulgarian a Russian, simply because he is a citizen of the Soviet Complex."

She shrugged it off. "It's all very uncultured, such things," she said, motioning him toward the couch. "It will be much better when we are all one world-wide Soviet Complex, and there are no such things as nationalities."

He inwardly shuddered at that idea, wanting to be a member of the Soviet Complex like he wanted several more holes in the vicinity of his ears, but held his peace and took his seat.

Catherina smoothed over to the small bar—smoothed could be the only word. She walked like a professional model, or perhaps a ballet dancer. He wondered if she had ever studied ballet, which was quite possible since she came from the Mecca of ballet. His mouth was dry, just looking at her.

She said, over her shoulder, "Are you sure that I'm not, what is the Yankee . . . uh, that is, American phrase, twisting your arm, in view of your beliefs in moderation?"

He cleared his throat. "Oh, no. No. I indulged very little at the party."

"Champagne?"

The inevitable goddamned champagne. The Russkies seldom drank anything at all but champagne and vodka. But he said, not wanting to place even the slightest of obstacles in the progress of the evening, "Excellent."

She returned with two glasses of the bubbly wine, handed him one, and took her place across from him.

Catherina said accusingly, "If you don't stop staring at me like that, I'll put something on over my . . . bosom. Don't women in the States have breasts?"

"Oh, sorry," he said, clearing his throat and bringing his eyes up to her face. And then, in an attempt at gallantry, "Not as spectacular as yours."

She said, "Thank you," and then, "Cheers, cheers, as you Americans say."

He had never heard that as an American toast, but he said, "Cheers, cheers," and they both drank.

She made a rueful mouth and said, as though in amusement, "You know, I have a confession to make to you."

He looked at her.

She said, "In spite of all I said in Malaga, on the tapa hunt, about not wanting to roll in the hay. Well . . . when I saw you take up Vovo's challenge . . . for me. I . . . well, I . . . felt regrets."

The cold went through him.

He stuttered, "I beg your pardon?" This simply couldn't be happening.

She laughed in self-deprecation. "Despite your feelings about moderation, and meekness, and well . . . uh, moderation in all things. I . . . well, I decided I wanted to spend this last night in Spain . . . well, with you."

"Holy smokes," he said.

He hurried to his feet, almost forgetting to put the glass of wine down, and almost stumbling over the rug in getting around to her.

She laughed as she shot to her own feet and slipped into his arms. "Mike, oh Mike," she said as he kissed her in such a way that Old Man Hemingway would have been proud of him.

Catherina's full mouth had been constructed with kissing in mind, without doubt. They stood there and proved that fact to the satisfaction of both of them. He had one of her full half-globes in the palm of his right hand, and hated the fact that their position was such that he couldn't be utilizing his left hand for the same purpose. He could feel the nipple hardening. Catherina was obviously far from frigid.

She said, finally, "The bedroom is in here," and, taking him by the hand, she led the way.

There were French windows leading off onto the terrace, which overlooked the moonlit sea. The moon was almost full. She didn't turn on the lights; the moon provided all the light they needed. It couldn't have been a more romantic setting for first love if it had been designed by Hollywood. It was a perfect set.

She came into his arms again for a brief moment and then stood back and with a very slight smile began to disrobe for him. She did it very slowly, deliberately provocatively. Mike had seen her, of course, in the briefest of bikini type bathing suits—or less—and so was prepared for her just-short-of-lush figure. But he sucked in breath when she was fully nude. Her pubic hair was almost, not quite, as blonde as that on her head. Most blondes, it had been his experience, were more apt to be dark there. Catherina was not only blond but the shock was abundant, another thing that Mike Edwards had always liked in a woman.

She posed a moment for him, proudly, knowing he would like that, her arms at her sides, the palms of her hands slightly out, somewhat like a Siamese dancer. He had never been so aroused.

She said softly, "Do you like me? Would you like to . . . have me?"

His voice was hoarse. "Yes, Yes, you are perfect, Catherina."

She sat on the side of the bed and said in mock accusation. "But you remain fully clothed. You'll have to get out of that . . . monkey suit, won't you? It doesn't seem tailored with the act of . . . love, in mind. Here, let me help you."

Her shapely, soft hands began fumbling with the unfamiliar hooks and buttons of the matador's costume. Mike shucked out of the jacket, tossed it to one side, not noticing if it hit the chair he aimed at or not.

When he was stripped, she complimented him. "My, my," she said. "Do you think I dare?" It most certainly didn't hurt his male ego.

As nude as she, he sat down next to her.

"Kiss me," she murmered sensuously.

He began to bend, but she said. "Not there, silly. You can do that later, if that's one of the things you like. It is one of the things I like, very much, though I do not often do it. But for now, kiss me on the mouth. I find you Americans very apt at kissing."

He gently ran his hand over her slightly rounded belly

and then over a hip, as he kissed her. Her body was absolutely silken.

"How many Americans have you kissed, to be able to come to a decision such as that?" he said heavily, as he took her lips again.

"Only one," she murmered. "You."

He pushed her gently onto her back. They hadn't even taken the time to turn down the bed clothing, but that could come later—if it was ever necessary to come. Such matters were not important in the urgency of the situation.

"What can I do to make you happy?" he said, still hoarse. He couldn't keep his hands from her crotch, his lips from her nipples.

"Anything you do will make me happy—except if you take too long. I'm . . . I'm raging for you. Please, put a pillow under my hips. I want all of you . . . all the way in. I can't stand it."

That direction accomplished, he leaned over her for a moment, admiring her female body, her ultimately feminine body.

She grasped his erection in her hand and murmured, "Is this for me, darling? All of it?"

"All of it." He descended upon her slowly.

She directed his entry, and then arched up almost as though desperately. Catherina obviously loved the act of love. "Oh, slowly," she moaned. "Deeply, but slowly. I want this first one to last ever so long. Oh, that feels so terribly good."

She was a talker. One more thing in her favor, so far as Mike was concerned. It gave him an added excitement, gasping, moaning and talking her pleasure as he performed with her.

Mike Edwards was far from a novice in the field of

sex. But he had never been so moved as by this girl. It nearly seemed as though it was his first time; his first *real* time. He judged himself carefully, timing himself by her little moans and her gasps of pleasure and by the rapidity of her movements. He was able to bring them to orgasm simultaneously and she gave a small shriek as she felt it coming.

They stretched out on their backs and relaxed, touching only to the extent of holding hands.

He said, "Do you have a full-time male friend in Moscow?"

"No," she told him. "And you? Do you have a fiancée in America? Or anywhere else, for that matter? Jealousy is a bit ridiculous, under the circumstances, but I feel I will be jealous if you answer yes."

"No," he said, quite truthfully. "There is no one. Catherina, somehow or other I'm going to come to Moscow."

She laughed ruefully. "Mike you fool. You told me you were going to return to the United States and take—what did you call it?—Holy Orders."

He wouldn't give up. "Then you could come to America," he said.

She shook her head. "Mike, I'm a production secretary in films. My job is in the Soviet Complex. I couldn't get work in your country."

"I could support you," he said stubbornly.

"On the pay of a student minister and then a beginning minister?"

Damn it. He had burnt his bridges behind him, telling her he was to take Holy Orders. He couldn't reveal the truth of the situation to her now. No, not even to Catherina.

She reached over and began to caress him. She whispered, "Have you rested long enough?'" Although he was already proving that he had.

She said, "How would you like to do it this time? Do you have some special way you like?" Her voice was a sensuous whisper. "Do you want me to go into the bath and wash myself so that you can do what you wanted to do before?"

His voice was so thick he could hardly talk. "Yes," he croaked. "We both will."

XII

Mike saw her off in the morning, on the tourist plane, kissing her thoroughly before she boarded. The other Russkies cheered sympathetically, but there were tears in Catherina's eyes, and his own face held desperation. Mike Edwards realized he had never been in love before; and now it was already over.

He said his goodbyes to Nick, Ana, and various of the others he had learned to know fairly well during their two weeks in Torremolinos.

Vovo Chernozov, cold sober, for once, was the last. He shook hands. "Mike," he said, very sincerely, "if you ever come to the Soviet Complex you must look me up. We will have a fine time together and I will take you to a match so that you can see me wrestle Turkoman style. My exhibition last night was not so good, as you will remember."

Mike laughed as best he could. "It's a date," he said.

He looked up at the plane. Catherina was waving

through a window. He waved back, but then had to retreat as the plane readied for taxiing off.

He met the incoming plane of the new batch of tourists and went through his routine of giving them a short rundown on their two weeks vacation. It was a standard affair and amounted to a little speech that he delivered in the waiting room. They were the usual, typical, Russkies, some of them already drunk from the booze they'd had on the airplane. Then, in the buses hired for the occasion, he had them driven into Torremolinos and distributed to the various hotels where they had their reservations.

After he had them all settled in, he went to the Hotel Espadon, where Frank Jones was staying, and looked the American up. It was almost noon by now and Jones was to be found in the bar, nursing his first bottle of beer of the day.

Mike said, "Let's go on up to your room. We have some preliminary plans to make, and this is a bit too public."

"That we have, laddy-buck, that we have," Jones said, finishing his beer. "Let's go."

They took the elevator to the NATO man's floor and entered his room. Mike immediately crossed over to the TV phone and dialed his London offiees. Frank Jones, looking at him quizzically, sat in one of the more comfortable chairs, if any Spanish chairs are comfortable.

When his immediate boss's face faded in, Mike came immediately to the point. He said, "Mr. Fremont, I have to resign, as of right now. You'll have to send another man down soonest to take over Torremolinos."

"What!" the other sputtered. "You can't do that. You're signed up for at least the balance of the season. Nobody else knows Torremolinos."

"I can't help it. I've been drafted," Mike told him. "Get a man in here immediately who speaks Spanish and Russian. I'll wait around until he arrives and tell him some of the local ropes. So long."

The other began a wail of protest, but Mike simply flicked the phone off. He turned back to Frank Jones.

Jones said, "Okay. We're underway, eh? We'd better get on up to London and check in with my NATO supervisors."

Mike looked at him. "Are you crazy?"

"What's the matter?"

Mike was impatient. "Did you think we were going to tell everybody and his brother about this?" he said sarcastically. "It would leak back to the Russkies before the week was out. They've undoubtedly got agents ass deep all through NATO."

Jones said indignantly, "Well, we can't do it all by ourselves. This is going to involve hundreds of people, the way you describe it. Possibly thousands. They're all going to have to be in on it."

"Like hell they are," Mike said, his voice grim. "Now, you say you're from NATO, just who is your boss?"

"I'm not really NATO myself, just on assignment to them temporarily. I'm an operative of the Bureau of International Investigation, working directly under Lawrence Bigelow."

"Bigelow, eh?" Mike said thoughtfully, running a thumb nail along the bottom of his chin. "I've heard about him, of course. Cloak and dagger. All right. We'll go see him. Him and the President. Otherwise, we stay mum until they've okayed it."

"The President," Jones said sourly. "It's about as easy to see him as it is to get an interview with Andrei Zorin, Number One, in the Kremlin."

"If this project is as important as you say it is," Mike Edwards told him, "he'll see us all right, all right. Otherwise he can stick the whole thing up his butt."

His Horizonal Holidays relief turned up on the morning plane the next day, and Mike Edwards spent the balance of the day checking the man out. The other was aghast at the short time involved in his instructions. He wanted Mike to stay at least the week out. He had never been in Torremolinos before, though he had worked with the Russkies in Sicily and in the Canary Islands, and spoke Spanish as well as Russian. Mike told him it was impossible and did what he could to lighten the other's load.

The following morning, he and Frank Jones took plane for Greater Washington. There had been no difficulty in getting in to see Lawrence Bigelow, for long years head of the biggest hush-hush bureau in Greater Washington. Jones had put a call through to him while still on the trans-Atlantic plane and the appointment had been arranged. Mike Edwards began to suspect that the somewhat colorless appearing Frank Jones carried more clout than had at first been indicated. Bigelow was in the higher echelons of government, but due to the nature of his department was seldom heard about, seldom in the news, and the usual story was that it was practically impossible to get through to him.

At the international airport at which their supersonic landed, they rent an aircushion car and drove on into Greater Washington.

Mike Edwards wasn't acquainted with the city and Jones gave him a running commentary as they progressed. The Lincoln Memorial, the Washington Monument, the White House, the Capitol Building, so on and so forth. He informed his companion that even the building in which the Bureau of International Investigation was housed was largely unknown. Jones estimated that nine-tenths of American citizens weren't even aware that such a bureau existed.

They pulled into a ramp which led to the underground parking area of the building, and came up to the check-out officers guarding it. They were a tough looking squad with enough in the way of firearms to have stopped a company.

Frank Jones said dourly, "I've known the sergeant here for at least ten years, but that doesn't make any difference. We're still treated like complete strangers."

The sergeant, a gun in his hand, said, "Your identifications, please."

Frank and Mike both handed over their identification cards. Frank Jones said, "We have appointments with the Chief."

The sergeant checked, then handed back the cards and said, "Fingerprints, please," presenting a portable screen, of a type that Mike Edwards had never seen before. They put their fingers of the right hand on the screen.

Mike said to the sergeant, mildly, "You wouldn't have a record of me. I was a professor in a university the last time I was in the States."

The sergeant said flatly, "We have the prints of every citizen of the United States, and several million people who aren't citizens, including those of Number One, in the Kremlin."

He flicked some buttons and stared into another device with which Mike was completely unfamiliar and then said, "Yes, gentlemen. Please pass. Mr. Jones, how are things going?"

"Fine, Pete," Frank said. "It's nice to be back home. The beer's lousy in Spain."

They drove on into the maw of the office building, parked and headed for the elevator bank. The elevator identity screen checked them and they proceeded to the thirteenth floor, the sanctum sanctorum of the Bureau of International Investigation, and were checked out only once more before being able to go on.

Mike said, in protest, "Holy smokes, do you check everybody like this?"

"That's right, everybody. Even the chief has to go through the whole routine every time he enters the building."

"It gets a little on the ridiculous side," Mike said. "You spend half your energies checking or being checked. And if you can't trust your bureau head, Bigelow, who can you trust?"

Frank Jones looked at him. "Suppose this happened. Suppose the Russkies, or whoever, rang in a spittin' image of Lawrence Bigelow. Suppose they kidnapped or killed the real Bigelow and substituted the dead ringer. Can you imagine how much damage such a substitute could do?"

"Cloak and dagger," Mike muttered.

They made their way through a forest of desks, clattering IBM machines, and other office equipment, in the long office room that extended before the inner offices of Lawrence Bigelow.

They eventually reached the Chief's office, and the identity screen picked them up. The door opened and they filed on through into the largest office Mike Edwards could off hand ever remember being in. Evidently, Lawrence Bigelow failed to stint himself. The massive furniture was of the best, you had to plow through the rug, and on the wall was a Rembrandt which was obviously original.

The espionage-counter-espionage head looked up at their entry.

He said, "Hello, Frank. And you must be Professor Edwards." He didn't bother to come to his feet for handshakes or any of the other amenities.

He must have been at least in his middle sixties, Mike decided, and looked a damn sight better on his very seldom TV broadcasts than he did in person. He was a stocky, heavy jowled man, with unfriendly eyes and unfriendly manner. However, he seemed to have a certain rapport with Jones. Once again, Mike came to the conclusion that Frank was higher in the echelons than he had suspected.

"Sit down," Bigelow said.

They sat.

Lawrence Bigelow said, tapping a sheaf of papers on the littered desk before him, "I've been going through your dossier, Professor."

"Just call me mister, now," Mike demured. "The professor is gone with the wind."

The head of America's top cloak and dagger bureau looked at him. "Don't crack wise with me."

Mike Edwards came to his feet and said, "Fuck you," turned and headed for the door. Obviously, he wasn't going to be able to work with this character.

Jones was shaking his head in gentle reproof, looking at his superior. He said mildly, "No . . . Chief."

Bigelow said, "Come back here, goddammit."

"Screw you," Mike told him, still heading for the door.

Lawrence Bigelow said to Frank, "What's the matter with this stupid son of a bitch?"

Frank said mildly, "He's an honest man. I haven't seen one for years."

Mike's hand was on the doorknob.

Bigelow, as though it killed him to say it, said, "Listen, for crissakes, you touchy son of a bitch, come back and at least argue with me."

"Screw you," Mike said, wrenching the door open. He was getting more sore by the minute at the way the other talked.

The other roared at him. "You're in my den, Buster. You come back here and sit down, or I'll have half a dozen of my heavies on you so fast you won't be able to count them. I'll have you stuck away somewhere so you won't get out until Panama freezes over.

Frank said, "Better come back, Mike. Just for the present, at least."

Mike Edwards turned around and returned to his chair. He said coldly, "I still say, fuck you, Bigelow. Now speak your piece."

"Speak *my* piece?" The flabbergasted bureau head looked at Jones in amazement.

Frank had been going through this, legs crossed, in complete detachment.

"You guys ought to get to know each other," he said. You're both impossible. I wish the hell I'd become a violin player, like my dear old mother wanted."

Lawrence Bigelow glowered at his subordinate, then again at Mike. He took several deep breaths and said, "All right. Let's start all over again." He grabbed a prehistoric looking briar pipe from a pipe rack on the desk and dragged a pound can of Sir Walter Raleigh toward him.

While he packed the pipe, he said to Frank Jones, "What the hell is up?"

Frank said, "Mike, here, thinks he has an answer to the Russkie tourist problem. He thinks he has a way of getting them to stay home."

His chief opened a box of kitchen matches and lit up, peering through the smoke first at Frank, then at Mike Edwards.

He looked back at Frank again. "And what do you think?"

"I think possibly he's got something. I think it's a long chance, but probably worth trying. God knows, nobody else has come up with anything at all."

Bigelow said to Mike, "Sorry I sounded off." He didn't look or sound as though he was sorry. "So what's the plan you've dreamed up?"

Mike Edwards had cooled down. At least to where he decided since he'd come this far, on top of resigning from his job, he might as well go into his song and dance.

He went over his scheme, elaborating upon it beyond the point he had with Jones. While he was talking, the other's pipe went out several times and he lit up over and over again. He was a match smoker, as could be seen by the pile of burnt out matches in his ash tray.

When Mike was finally through and had lapsed into silence, Bigelow ran his right hand over his fat jowls, grimaced and shook his head. "For Christ sakes," he growled. "A new religion."

Mike began to come to his feet again, his lips beginning to go pale.

Bigelow said hurriedly, "Sit down, sit down. I didn't say anything. Did you expect me to stand up and do a dance? Do you think it will work?"

"It's worth a try," Mike said sitting. "From what Frank says, you're clutching at straws and there aren't any others to clutch. From what I saw of those Russkies in Torremolinos, it stands a chance."

The other tried to relight the pipe, still once again, scowled and looked down into the bowl to check the tobacco level, and then put the briar back on the pipe rack.

He thought about it. Mike and Frank Jones sat there, wordlessly.

The bureau chief took in about a gallon of air, sighed and said, "Okay. I'll arrange a meeting with the President, Senator Murray, Freguson of the FBI, Smithers of the CIA, the British and French Ambassadors . . ."

Mike was shaking his head. "No," he said.

Bigelow looked at him. "What do you mean, no? I can't make such a decision on my own."

Mike said, "I mean no. The President and possibly the current chief of NATO whoever the hell it is. But on no account anybody else."

Bigelow looked at Jones. "Is he around the bend?"

Frank recrossed his legs. "Mike's got the idea that if the story spreads around it will leak to the Kremlin, then all bets will be off. He's probably right, but it doesn't make much sense to me. Thousands of people are going to have to be in on this before it's operational."

Mike was still shaking his head. "Nobody is going to be in on it except we three, the President and the head of NATO. And that's too goddamned many. You see, we're going to play it straight. It's something like the Manhattan Project during the Second World War. A thousand different manufacturing firms were working on this aspect, or that, but none of them had the vaguest idea what the end product was going to be. Only a handful of scientists at the very top had the whole picture. That's the way we're going to operate; only four or five people will have the full picture."

XIII

Mike Edwards and Frank Jones were quartered in the New Greater Washington Hotel, a swank hi-rise usually patronized by VIPs of the diplomatic corps, by American government bigwigs, and by wealthy businessmen in town to check matters out with their lobbyists, or whatever.

The suite was king-sized. Two bedrooms, two baths, living room, complete with a small bar, an office.

Mike pursed his lips. "Holy smokes. There's nothing this lush in Torremolinos. Why pays for it? The condition my bankroll is in, I couldn't rent it for a good half hour."

"It goes on my expense account," Jones told him, taking his two bags into one of the bedrooms and then coming out and heading for the bar.

"No wonder there's a depression, with third rate government employees putting digs like these on the expense account." Mike picked up his own bags and took them into the other bedroom, then returned to flop down on one of the two couches.

"We're not third rate employees," Jones told him, coming up with a can of Danish beer, and finding an opener for it. "We're either first rate, or no rate at all. That remains to be seen. Want a beer?"

"Not now. Do you think Bigelow bought it?"

Jones thought about it while taking a sip of the brew. "Damned if I know. We'll find out tomorrow at the White House."

"Expense account, eh?" Mike said. "How big an expense account?"

"Practically unlimited on this assignment."

Mike rubbed his hands together. "Great. Let's go. I've never been in Greater Washington before. For once I can be a tourist instead of going batty herding them around."

"Let's go where?" Jones said warily

"Where do you think?" Mike said in indignantion. "In search of wine, women and song. In search of the fleshpots of this Babylon on the Potomac."

"Nope," Jones told him, finishing off the beer and heading back to the bar for a fresh one.

Mike looked at him.

Jones said, "You're under wraps, at least until a decision has been made on your scheme. I've been ordered not to let you out of my sight, and to keep you off the streets. Some newspaperman might spot you and wonder what the noted economist Michael Edwards is doing in Greater Washington."

"Nuts," Mike said. "Nobody remembers me. I didn't make as big a splash as all that. And what I did make was back in New Mexico."

"No nightclubbing," Jones told him, opening his beer can.

"Then bring me a drink, damn it. Anything but champagne."

In the morning, Frank Jones received a phone call. He said, "Yes, sir," a couple of times then flicked off the TV phone and turned to Mike, who was finishing breakfast at a small table the waiter had set up for the purpose.

"Okay," the Bureau of International Investigations man said. "We're on our way. The Chief will meet us at the White House"

Mike finished his coffee. "So, it wasn't as hard to get an appointment with President Clark as all that, eh?" He came to his feet, and tossed his napkin to the table.

There was a limousine waiting for them at the hotel's door. In the front seat was a uniformed chauffeur and another man whose air indicated quite definitely that he was a bodyguard. He got out of the car and opened the car's back door for them.

Jones greeted him. "Hi, Jerry," he said. Then to Mike, "Secret Service. You're getting the old red carpet treatment."

"Very impressive," Mike muttered. "Let's just hope they don't pull it out from under me."

The guards at the White House entry had obviously been informed of their arrival. The huge iron gates swung open before them, swung closed after they had sped through. The driver circled the White House to a side entrance and came to a halt. The Secret Serviceman got out and opened the door for Mike and Frank and stood to one side, looking alertly about, in spite of the fact that they were on the White House grounds.

Frank Jones led the way to the door, which opened at their approach. Two more heavies stepped out and looked at them narrowly. However, evidently security was less here than at the building which housed Lawrence Bigelow's Bureau, to Mike's surprise. One of the two nodded at Frank Jones and said, "Hello, Frank. The President is expecting you."

He looked at Mike and said, "We were told not to speak to your companion. We don't even know his name."

"Good," Frank said. "Let's go."

They entered the White House and started down a lengthy succession of corridors. Mike was amazed at the size of the building. He'd had no idea it was this big from the photos, newsreels and such that he had seen.

They finally reached a door which one of the Secret Service men rapped on discreetly. It was opened by what was obviously a secretary, a male secretary. Frank and Mike entered, the latter feeling slightly apprehensive. He had never met a chief of state before.

The room was obviously a minor office, rather than the President's formal one Why they were meeting here, Mike didn't know. Possibly something to do with added security.

President Thomas Clark was seated at the desk, flanked by Lawrence Bigelow on one side, and a uniformed middle-aged man on the other. Clark, of course, was immediately recognized. A handsome, smiling, alert man, who won half his votes purely because of his beautiful TV image. His boyish grin alone captured more of the woman vote than anything of its type since Eisenhower.

And his charm went beyond physical appearance. He was every inch the politician. He came to his feet and held out a hand to Mike, enthusiastically. "Academician Edwards," he said, and his voice was hearty. "It's a real pleasure to meet you."

Mike blinked, shook and said, "Thank you, Mr. President."

President Clark said, turning to indicate the others to each side of him, "You've met Larry Bigelow. And this is General MacHenry, of NATO. Ted, shake hands with Academician Michael J. Edwards."

The general shook. He was stereotyped to the point of looking as though he had come out of a Pentagon mold. Straight as the proverbial ramrod, graying of hair, aggressive of eye, and stern of mouth. Inwardly, Mike Edwards thanked lucky stars that he wasn't a colonel under this one.

The President looked at the male secretary who had opened the door for the newcomers and said, "That will be all, Duncan. Under no circumstances, short of the building burning down, are we to be interrupted."

"Yes, Mr. President." Duncan turned and left.

The President seated himself again and looked at Mike and Frank. "Please be seated, gentlemen."

They found chairs.

The President said, "Shall we immediately get to cases? Larry has given me only the briefest summary of what you have in mind. Frankly, I am somewhat taken aback."

Mike said, "Sir, is there any chance, whatsoever, that this room might be bugged?"

Thomas Clark frowned at him. "Certainly not."

"We can't run any chances of what we're going to be saying leaking out. Are you bugging it yourself? That is, is our conversation being taped?"

The President scowled at him this time. He said, "Why, yes, of course. For my records."

Mike shook his head, somewhat surprised at his own

temerity. "No, sir. How many hands does a tape cut for you go through, before all is done?"

The President cocked his head. "I see what you mean." He flicked a switch on the desk and said, into some microphone that Mike didn't even see, "There is no tape to be cut of this conversation." He turned back to Mike Edwards, "Very well, Academician. Let us proceed."

Originally, Mike Edwards had figured on a minor role for himself in the evangelistic attack on the Soviet Complex. Preferably as a missionary in the Moscow area. But it didn't work out that way. The more acceptance his basic plan received the more power was shifted into his hands

Actually, at that first meeting with the President, the NATO man and Bigelow, he had been dismayed to find the extent to which they needed him. Even the President, not to speak of the other two, still operated with the old Good-Guys-Versus-the-Bad-Guys mentality. They had too little knowledge of the workings of their own politico-economic system and negative knowledge of the Soviet Complex. It was all black and white with them. He was appalled that men with as little background as this were at the head of the nation.

He had gone over his plan in detail, sketching out the whole thing. But the general, in particular, couldn't get it through his head that this whole dumping of manufactured goods wasn't a sinister scheme on the part of the Kremlin.

"Look," Mike had said at one point. "For half a century the world has been in the Second Industrial Revolution. The revolution of the computer and automated factories. Man's age-old problem has finally been solved—the production of sufficient food, clothing and shelter, medical needs and education for *everyone*. Different groups accomplished it by somewhat different methods —the United States and the Soviet Complex, Mexico and Sweden, Japan and Brazil, Yugoslavia and Israel—but at this stage, it's been achieved by just about all."

The general had huffed, "But with that prime ingredient, *freedom* in the West."

Mike nodded. "Correct, but let's not read into that term more than is there It means various things and sometimes one man's freedom isn't another man's definition of it. Remember when we were using it most often at the height of the Cold War? The so-called 'free world' included Saudi-Arabia, Spain, Portugal, Formosa, South Korea and South Vietnam. Evidently, a country was 'free' simply because it was on our side, rather than with the Russkies. Actually freedom is never complete. Every society puts restrictions on the freedom of its people. The moment there is more than one person in a society, there are restrictions on the freedom of each individual. But that's not the important point. The thing is that even in those Cold War days everything was in a condition of flux. Scientific discoveries, breakthroughs in medicine, population explosion, fantastic industrial boom. And, above all, changes in society. The governments of every major nation on Earth were in a state of change."

Lawrence Bigelow had cleared his throat at that point and Mike turned on him.

"Who would contend that the administrations following Nixon were the same type of government as the administration of, say, Hoover? True enough we retained the outer symbols of classical capitalist democracy, but the inner changes taking place were fantastic."

"Ummm," the President said. "I was talking to the British Ambassador just the other day. He pointed out that Her Majesty's government has seen many changes in the past half century. What is called a Conservative today would have been considered a flame-snorting, left-wing Laborite before. The so-called Welfare State has developed far beyond the point ever dreamed of by the old Fabian Socialists. But, I must say, the changes taking place on the Soviet side are just as shaking."

"That's the point," Mike said, glad to see he was evidently winning Thomas Clark over. "The Russia of Stalin had little resemblance to that of Lenin. But the Russia of Khrushchev evolved even more. Nikita was hard put to run fast enough with those chubby short legs of his, to keep out in front of his rapidly changing politico-economic system, his developing New Class. And after Khrushchev? Well, the Old Bolshevik, complete with a bomb in one hand and a copy of the *Communist Manifesto* in his hip pocket, just had no place in the new Soviet Complex; he was as extinct as the economic Robber Baron of the American Nineteenth Century."

"What are you getting at?" the general had growled.

Mike laid it on the line. "If we're going to survive in this continuing battle for men's minds, we've got to recognize the changes that have taken place and are taking place. Recognize them and adapt to them. If we can do this better than the Russkies, then we'll have a considerable advantage. As it is now, they're as befuddled about us as we are about them."

At the end they had wound up giving him carte blanche for all practical purposes. Frank Jones was assigned to be his assistant and his liaison man with the Bureau of International Investigation through which all funding would go, secretly. Mike Edwards was granted an annual salary of $35,000 and Jones $25,000; a considerably larger amount than either had ever expected to earn. Mike was to make his reports through Bigelow to the President, and they were to be kept to a minimum, for the sake of as tight security as they could manage. The President was to keep in touch with General MacHenry, the sole NATO representative to be in on the secret.

XIV

The initial meeting with the President, Bigelow and General MacHenry had taken a full six hours. Mike Edwards was exhausted by the time he and Frank had returned to their suite. All of his instincts were to flop immediately into bed. But time was the important thing at this stage of the game. He had won every point. They had conceded him his whole program. Now he had to put up or shut up.

He sat down in the living room, took a deep breath and said, "All right. Pull up a drink, assistant, and start assisting."

Frank Jones went over to the small bar, fished around in the refrigerator and came up with a bottle of Tuborg beer. He popped the cork, poured the brew into a pewter tankard, whilst saying, "Now that I'm rich, I could afford more expensive beer But the trouble is, this is the best brew going, no matter what you pay for it. The wealthy have their problems." He returned with the drink to sit across from Mike.

He said, "All right, shoot."

"Shoot it is," Mike said. "From now on in, I don't want to be seen either entering the White House or your Bureau of International Investigations. I'm still under wraps as far as they're concerned. Undercover. I don't want some smart assed Russkie agent wondering about me and looking me up. So you'll do the legwork. Like Bigelow said, you're the liaison man."

"Makes sense," Frank nodded, taking a plug at his beer.

Mike said, "First of all, I want an island where we can stash a half-dozen or so prominent men for a year or two. A place where they'll be under the tightest security. No communication with the mainland. The people who take care of them and maintain the security will also have no contact with the mainland. It will possibly be a little complicated to set up their supply system, but I'm sure you have people who can work out an arrangement."

Frank was staring at him. "Have you gone completely around the corner?" he demanded. "You can't do that in a a democracy. Besides, why?"

"You'll see later," Mike told him. "Yes, you can do it in a democracy. I didn't say we were going to kidnap them. It'll be voluntary on their part. We'll offer them money. All the money they want."

"Offer who money, for Christ's sakes?"

"That brings us to the second of the things I need done. I want you to round up for me the dozen or so most celebrated scholars of comparative religion in this country. Just to be sure they'll come, you might get letters off to them from the White House, signed by the President. A request that they come to Greater Washington for an interview."

"What in the hell."

Mike went over to the bar and poured himself a snifter glass of the stone age cognac there, and returned with it to his seat

"Then I want a seminary," he said.

"A seminary?"

"Yes, or some complex of buildings that can be quickly converted into one. A religious school, in short. And it'll have to be big enough for several hundred students. Stock its library with all sorts of religious crap. All sorts. Every religion."

He thought about it. "Oh, yeah. One other thing you better get to work on. I assume you've got Number One Priority in the National Data Banks?"

"I can get it through the Chief," Jones said.

"All right. Possibly this will take some time. I want to have the computers go through the dossiers of every man and woman in the country between the ages of twenty-five and forty. First pull all those who speak and read and write Russian, and the various other languages spoken in the Soviet Complex."

Frank looked his dismay and took down half of what remained of his beer "There'll be millions of them. Russian is the most popular language taught in high school and college now."

"I know," Mike said, inhaling the bouquet of the brandy. "Next pull all who have an I.Q. of over 120. No, you'd better make that 125."

"That'll eliminate a lot of them."

"Yes. From those remaining, pull all who are unemployed or who have low paying jobs. From the remaining pull those who are in good health and are good-looking physical specimens. From what's left, eliminate those who are *too* good looking. We don't want pretty girls, handsome men; what we're looking for are sincere, honest, motivated looking types. They don't have to be sincere, honest and motivated but they're going to have to *look* as though they are."

"Holy Jesus what are you looking for?"

"Students for my missionary school, of course. You'd better get jumping on these things first thing in the morning."

Frank looked at him sourly "What are you going to be doing while I'm dashing around rounding up religious scholars, a seminary, and a bunch of students."

Mike said with considerable aloof dignity. "I'm going to be meditating. Possibly contemplating my navel, that sort of thing. You never know where this religious kick might lead you."

Mike Edwards got a total turnout of fourteen religious scholars as a result of Jones' efforts.

He and Frank got them seated in the living room of his suite. They were all, of course, mystified. Most of them knew at least several of the others. And some time was spent in greetings. Mike Edwards waited it out.

When they were through, settled down and quiet, he looked at them, nodded, and said, "It is not necessary that you know my name. First of all, let me thank you, in the name of the President, for your response to his request."

"I thought we were to have a personal interview with President Clark," one of them scowled. "What is the meaning of all this?"

Mike held up a restraining hand. "In a moment, sir. First, let me ask you all a question. Are any of you religious? I am not requesting what creed you might believe in, any at all."

They stared at him.

He held his peace.

Several spoke at once, several in various ways asking what he meant by religion.

Monseigneur Fitzgerald, the only one present who wore robes, said coldly, "I am a member of the Society of Jesus, sir. Your question is an insult."

"It's not meant to be. Forgive me," Mike told him, holding up his hands in a request for silence. "Please, will you each indicate whether or not you believe in a Supreme Being and an afterlife?"

Eight hands went up of the fourteen. The remaining six looked at their colleagues in various degrees of amusement.

Mike stood. He said to the eight, "Thank you very much gentlemen. That is all we will require of you. All your expenses will be paid and whatever amount you feel you wish to request as payment for your time. Possibly you will wish to donate that amount to your church, or favorite charity. That is up to you."

Monseigneur Fitzgerald, Irish-like, was indignant. He sputtered, "Do you mean to tell us that we are not even to be told the reason for our being so cavalierly summoned to this ridiculous meeting?"

"I am afraid so Monseigneur," Frank Jones put in gently. "It is a matter of national security. Once again, thank you for coming. The President is thankful and has instructed me to so inform you."

It took another ten minutes to get the eight out. When it was over, Mike Edwards felt like wiping his forehead with his handkerchief, but refrained.

He looked at the six remaining; middleaged or elderly men, professors, writers, retired scholars. All, obviously, fascinated by the mystery of this. And all, evidently either atheists or agnostics.

Mike took a deep breath and said, "Gentlemen, your country needs you."

"I am not a patriot," one said testily.

Mike looked at him. He didn't recall the name, but he could learn their names later The other was the type who would speak testily. Undoubtedly, he went through life being testy.

Mike said, "You need not be. But we arrive at this next point. If any, or all, of you gentlemen take me up on my proposition, you will be rewarded beyond your dreams of avarice—assuming that scholars such as yourselves have dreams of avarice."

One of them laughed slightly at that, a wry quality there.

Mike went on. "But it will mean seclusion for a year, two years, possibly even more. The matter is of such importance that you will be allowed no communication with the outside world. You will be quartered, in seclusion, on one of the smaller Hawaiian islands in luxury. I might add, until the duration of the emergency which now faces the country. You will have every facility. Any books, anything, period, that you require to continue your studies, or whatever else you wish to do to pass your time. But you will be completely cut off from the rest of the world."

"Completely divorced from our families?" one blurted.

Mike shook his head "Not necessarily. You may bring your families to the island, but then, they too will be in complete seclusion for the duration."

Another broke in. "This is a matter of extreme national importance, you say?"

"It involves the survival of our nation as we know it," Frank Jones said.

One of them stood. He was a grim-faced, leathery man in his early sixties. "I want no part of this," he said.

Mike said, "Frank."

Frank escorted the other to the door.

Mike Edwards looked at the remaining five. "Very well, gentlemen. This is your last opportunity to back out. From now on in, you're committed. All bets are down."

One of them, Mike vaguely remembered his name as Altschuler, said, "Very well. Now what is your proposition, Mr.——"

"My name isn't of importance," Mike said "You are all in?"

They all nodded.

"All right. The proposition is this. We want to invent, I suppose the best term would be, a new religion."

They looked at him as though he was mad.

Mike took a deep breath. "There are some ramifications. For one thing, it must make sense. The people to whom it must be appealing, are not Bible-belt Americans from the South. Or bigoted farmers from Iowa. They average high in education. They are, largely, not fools."

"What do you mean, make sense?" one demanded. Mike couldn't remember his name either.

"Exactly that," Mike told him. "We want a new religion, but it cannot have such nonsense in it as, say, a heaven and hell."

The testy one said, "Why do you think the conceptions of heaven and hell are nonsense? I do not say I disagree with you but I'm interested in your reasoning."

Mike nodded. "They're nonsense because both are impossible. You can't have perpetual pleasure nor perpetual pain. Both pleasure and pain are contrasts. Suppose, after I have gone to my reward, they throw me into a fire of sulphur and brimstone for all eternity. I admit it might hurt considerably at the beginning, but after the first thousand years or so, I rather doubt that I would be much distressed. The same with the perpetual pleasure of paradise. I doubt if whatever the pleasure consists of would be much fun after the first ten thousand years or so."

Altshuler said, "Those who differ with you would point out that the material you does not go to either heaven or hell, but your immortal soul. It would have differing requirements, a different viewpoint on pleasure and pain."

"More nonsense," Mike said definitely. "I, as an individual, have various attributes. I like to eat. I like to drink good booze. I like to sleep with beautiful women. I like to play poker. I like a good cigar. I dislike physical violence. All these and other things in multitudes make up the identity that is me. Take them away and it is no longer me."

All five were looking at him thoughtfully.

"Very well, what else?" one said.

Mike said, "In the past, most new religions that have come down the pike have been founded by devoted fanatics. And, since they were fanatics, many, if not all, of their teachings were fanatical. Take Mohammed, the Prophet. He believed in efrits and djinn, and worked them into his religion of Islam.

"This time, we're not going to be fanatical. We're going to select the best of the teachings of all the religions of the past, and, hopefully, add a few more of our own. And we're going to build a new religion that will appeal to *modern* man. Most of the great religions of the world were conceived of two thousand or more years ago; Buddhism and Hinduism, even longer. Judaism,

Christianity and Mohammedism were all conceived by nomads in the Middle East. Such items as the Jews not eating shellfish made a lot of sense in the times of Moses, since they had no refrigeration, and nothing spoils so quickly in a hot climate than shellfish. But it doesn't make sense now. Gentlemen, we want a modern religion that a present day person can identify with."

He looked about at them. "Very well, that is the basic idea."

The testy one said, "But what is this so-called new religion to be about? And why are we to do it? What is accomplished? And why the secrecy, this whole matter of our being secluded for a year or more?"

Mike said, "The why of it is top secret and that is the reason you must be put off on this remote island. Later, perhaps, I do not know, but you might be completely informed and the plaudits of the nation will be due you. Time will work this out. Although it will be new, we will call it the Old Time Religion Church. For some reason, people feel confidence in the belief that their moral codes, religions and such, go way back. The strongest tenets will be moderation, meekness, the simple life, the pleasures of home and the family. We might even work in a slight amount of xenophobia and nationalism. The love of one's own country to the point where one does not wish to travel to other lands."

He wound it up. "I'll work with all this with you in detail"

The testy one said, without his usual testiness, "You know, I am not completely opposed to the project. A great deal of what you have said makes considerable sense. If people want religion, at least they should have a well thought out one. And who could think it out better than we five here?"

Mike said, unctuously, "Gentlemen, I have complete confidence in your abilities." He added dryly, "If anyone in the world could come up with a viable new religion, certainly you five agnostics and atheists, who have spent your lives studying religion, can."

XV

Mike Edwards and Frank Jones were over drinks again, this time seated in the small office of Mike's suite. They had both been working under pressure for several weeks now, and were beginning to show the strain. Mike was seldom out of the hotel.

On the desk was a long list of the potential Russian speaking missionary students who had been selected by the computers from the National Data Banks dossiers that were kept on every citizen of the nation. Suuposedly the dossiers were highly confidential, giving every bit of intimate information available. But the Old Time Religion Church project held top priority. It could snoop into anybody's privacy on a Presidential level.

Mike said, unhappily, "I'll have to interview each one of them personally, but meanwhile we have various odds and ends. I want you to sign up one of the advertising agencies to turn out some hymns. We'll want the most competent tunesmiths in Tin Pan Alley to work on them."

He thought about that aspect for a few moments. "Come to think of it, the Russkies are pretty music conscious. Could we dig up some really classical new hymns, something like Haydn used to knock out? Any American composers currently on the scene who could whomp up something really spiritual for the Old Time Religion Church?"

"No. The tops that we've reached in the past century are Irving Berlin and Cole Porter. Haydn, for Christ sakes."

Mike looked at him. "Where in the hell did you ever hear of Franz Josef Haydn?"

"Don't be a goddamned culture snob. I used to work as a pianist in a whorehouse. Whores are very sentimental."

Mike looked at him.

Frank said, "You know, it might be a good idea if we used old Russian folk song tunes as the background music. They'll be able to identify better."

"Good idea," Mike said. "Work on it."

He said, looking down at the notes on the desk, "As soon as my five double domes come up with our new theology we'll get books, pamphlets, brochures and throwaway leaflets printed. We'll need the best writers in the country to do them up, not a bunch of hacks. Damn it, it's too bad both Hemingway and Faulkner are dead. Then, of course, we'll have to have them translated into Russian."

"Yeah," Frank said. "It's too bad Tolstoy is dead, too. He could have written the stuff for you directly in Russian."

"Mind the humor," Mike told him. "It doesn't become you." He looked at his notes again. "Oh, yes. Just as soon as we have our gospel all smoothed out, I'm going to need TV time, prime time. An hour each Sunday."

Frank looked at him. "What in the hell for?"

Mike spoke reasonably. "This thing can't just spring into prominence overnight. We've got to build up to it. Bishop Michael J. Edwards will have to start spreading the message initially right here in the States. We'll leak it to the press that the Old Time Religion Church was first a very small denomination in the Middle West—we won't mention *where* in the Middle West—but that it has taken on and avalanched. Which reminds me. Line us up a half dozen of the top publicity agents. We're going to have to splash Bishop Edwards' kisser in every publication in the country, get him into all the columns and so forth."

Frank Jones finished his beer. "For Christ sakes, Mike. You might really make some converts, sincere converts."

"I'd better," Mike said grimly.

His partner was indignant. "But it's all a fake! You can't sucker the American people into a phoney religion. It's not . . . well, it's not ethical."

Mike looked at him strangely. "You still don't get it, do you? This isn't a fake, Frank. It's a damn good religion. It's going to have to be or the Russkies won't buy it. There's nothing wrong with teaching moderation, some of the best brains of all time have done so. And as far as the American people are concerned, it won't hurt them to practice a little of it. We're not as bad as the Russkies but we've come a long way from the virtues of a century ago."

Frank Jones shook his head, came to his feet and went into the other room for another bottle of Tuborg.

When he came back, Mike said, "Oh, yes. Another thing. I need some professors for the seminary. Some really top educators who can teach the Old Time Religion to my missionary students, as soon as we find out what the Old Time Religion is."

"How in the hell can we do that? You haven't converted anyone yet, professors or otherwise," Frank said in disgust.

"They don't have to believe in it. All they've got to do is teach it. We'll also have to have classes in speaking, advanced classes in Russian, classes in contemporary Soviet Complex life, so they'll know what they're getting into, all the rest of it. You'd better take in a few seminaries and find out what makes them tick."

"Oh, great," Frank said, pulling away at his beer.

Mike took in his notes again and muttered, "I guess we'd better wear black suits and reversed collars, Reverend. They give a certain authenticity to a religious worker."

"Reverend?" Frank said blankly.

"That's right. From now on, you're the Reverend Frank Jones, right hand man of Bishop Edwards."

"Jesus H. Christ," Frank protested. "The things I've done for my country."

The doorbell buzzed and Mike Edwards checked the identity screen.

"It's probably one of the students selected by the computers," Mike sighed. "The first to turn up so far. Show him in, Reverend, and mind your goddamned foul language while he's here."

Frank ditched his beer bottle and assumed a funeral parlor expression and went to the door.

He returned with a man of possibly thirty. Mike noted with satisfaction that the other was a sincere, clean cut type and undoubtedly of Nordic background. That had been another of the requirements, he'd worked into the computer selections. He suspected that it would be easier for the Russkies to identify with the northern races rather than, say, the Latins.

Frank said, "Bishop Edwards, this is Henry Matheson, one of the students selected for the scholarship."

Mike came around the desk and clasped the other by the hand heartily and said, "Congratulations, son. It is a pleasure to meet you."

The newcomer looked from Mike to Frank and back again. He said, "Students? Scholarship? What's all this about? In the mails I received a check large enough to pay my expenses here to Greater Washington and with a rather cryptic suggestion of an offer. I supposed it was a job. What's this Bishop bit?"

"Be seated, be seated, son." Mike told him. "I'll tell you all about it."

The other, bewildered, took a chair across the desk from Mike's place.

Mike Edwards came directly to the point. He said, "The Old Time Religion Foundation is awarding scholarships to those most suited for the first semester of the Old Time Religion Seminary for Missionaries."

The other gaped at him. "And *I* was picked?"

Mike looked down at his list on the desk. "That is correct, son. Of all the young men and women in America, you were one of the few hundred selected. Congratulations."

The other shook his head emphatically. "You must have the wrong Henry Matheson. Either that, or somebody is way off the beam. Me go to a seminary for missionaries? I'm an agnostic."

Mike smiled at him. "That is of no importance, my son. Perhaps by the time you have finished the course, you will see the light and remain on with the Old Time Religion as a missionary, spreading the light of the gospel of moderation."

"Not a chance, friend." Matheson began to come to his feet.

But Mike held up a restraining hand. "My son, the computers selected you from the National Data Banks. It is unlikely that they made a mistake. You have failed to enquire about the terms of the scholarship."

The other hesitated. "Terms? A scholarship is a scholarship, isn't it? Free tuition. I couldn't afford the other expenses involved even if I did take it."

Mike pretended to check his list again. He said, "Your dossier reveals that you are at present unemployed. The foundation is generously endowed. Not only are you given free tuition and all other expenses involved in your studies, but you receive regular pay which would be somewhat in excess of what you were making on your last job."

The other sank back into the chair he had just deserted. "Pay?" he said.

"Yes, of course," Mike said jovially. "We couldn't let our earnest students starve, could we? And then, at the end of the six month intensive course, if you took the missionary assignment, that pay would be doubled."

"But . . . but I told you I was an agnostic."

"Of no moment, my son," Mike said unctuously. "And perhaps you will be converted to the gospel once you have studied it, as I have said. The work is most important. This first class to graduate is scheduled to bring the good word to the Soviet Complex."

"A trip to the Soviet Complex, eh? All expenses paid, of course?"

"Of course. And a bonus for every month spent overseas."

The other cleared his throat. "When does this first semester of the new missionary school start?"

Frank Jones said, ever so smoothly, "Next week, but, particularly in view of your unemployed status, your pay would begin as of now. Perhaps you would like an advance of, say, a month's salary?"

When Henry Matheson had staggered out, a check in hand, a dazed expression on his face, the two looked after him.

Frank said, "One will get you ten that lad will become piously converted to the Old Time Religion Church before the month is out."

"No bet," Mike said. "Listen, I've just had another idea. Get hold of the biggies in clothing style design. We're going to start the Old-Fashioned Look. Spend a lot of dough on advertising. Spend as much as is necessary in all the media. This new style, for both men and women, will stress conservatism in dress, if not downright puritanism. The Russkies notoriously copy Western styles. It'll put them in a frame of mind to be receptive to the Old Time religion."

"Sounds good," Frank said. "There goes the bell again. Probably another of your scholarship students."

"Show him in, Frank."

Mike rubbed his hands in anticipation. So far, everything was shaping up.

XVI

Bishop Michael J. Edwards flew into Moscow approximately a year after his crash program had begun. He had been preceeded by the Reverend Frank Jones and a contingent of the first missionary seminary graduates. Others of the spreaders of the new gospel had been dispatched to other cities. Back at home, new classes were being taught in the various languages of the Soviet Complex ranging from Hungarian to several of the more widely spoken Siberian tongues. If nothing else, Mike was playing it thorough.

When he finally arrived at the capital city of the Soviet Complex, he found that Moscow offered him few surprises. He had already known that the mushrooming Russkie capital had surpassed even Tokyo in population. Books, TV and films had prepared him for the ultra-cleanliness of the streets, the beauty of the Kremlin and Red Square, the other squares and parks all over the city, the booming night clubs and good-time centers.

He was met at the Vnukovo airport by three of his

young missionaries and by several of the United States Embassy officials, all of whom had been instructed by their superiors to give his arrival a big play. After all, he was Michael J. Edwards, Bishop of the Old Time Religion Church and titular head of all missions abroad, including those in the Soviet Complex.

Of course, not even the State Department was acquainted with the real purpose of Mike's descending upon Moscow, but it didn't hurt to have the local embassy people backing him up. If nothing else, it would give him some prestige in the eyes of the Russkies. Perhaps he would have them throw him a big welcoming banquet. But no, that wouldn't fit in with the moderation pitch.

Even as he came down the ramp from the rocketplane which had brought him across the Atlantic, he noted with satisfaction that the aircushion cars belonging to the Western consular officials were in the new styles from Detroit. Black in color, ultra-austere in lines. The campaign toward simplicity and austerity was moving along at a satisfying clip. They'd had their work cut out getting Detroit to adapt the Old-Fashioned Look to auto design, in fact their advertising departments had torn out large swaths of hair, but the President pushed it through with promises of lower taxes.

A young man in black, and with reversed collar, was the first to pump his hand enthusiastically. "Bishop Edwards," he gushed, "you have no idea what a pleasure it is to greet you. I haven't seen you since your inspiring talk to the graduating class. Undoubtedly, you don't remember me. I'm David Masters. I'm to be your secretary-assistant, under the Reverend Jones, of course."

"Certainly I remember you, Reverend," Mike said severely. "One does not rise to the rank of Bishop in the Old Time Religion Church by being forgetful of the loyal missionaries in the field who are attempting to increase the number of the flock in the fold."

Hell, that came out pretty good, Mike felt. He was beginning to get the feel of this thing.

Others were coming up. Too many of them for Mike to retain any names. Well, that could come later. He shook hands all around, made with the usual banalities of greetings, and finally wound up in a black limousine, driven by a dark uniformed chauffeur. The Reverend David Masters piled in beside him.

Masters was gushing, "You'll be most gratified to find what progress we've been making. We . . ." He came to a halt suddenly and blinked at Mike.

"What's the matter?" Mike scowled at him.

"Why," the other said hesitantly, "it's nonsense, of course, but if I didn't know better I would have sworn I smell, ah, the demon rum on your breath."

Mike looked at him. Sometimes he wondered if it was a good idea to keep the lower echelons in complete ignorance of their real role. This one looked as though he was going to be a lulu to have around.

He said dryly, "The stewardess gave me something for airsickness. I have little knowledge about such medication, Brother, but I am sure she would not have administered it unless it had been recommended by the airline physicians. We must attack the use of alcohol in moderation, realizing that it has various medical uses."

"Why, of course, how ridiculous of me. Thank you for pointing out the correct path, Bishop."

Mike said piously, "Verily, he who seeks evil but finds it. Blessed are the trusting. *Genesis* XIX. 5."

The other whipped out a notebook and quickly scribbled into it. "What a wonderful useful quotation, Bishop Edwards," he gushed. Oh, he was a gusher, all right. It was going to be a chore getting used to having him around.

He wondered why Frank had picked this one as secretary. Probably because he wasn't very quick on the uptake and consequently would catch on that something wasn't fragrant about this whole missionary bit.

In actuality, Mike had pulled that quotation off the top of his head. He could no more have quoted chapter and verse from the Bible than he could have sprouted a halo.

He said severely, "And who is responsible for this ostentatious vehicle to pick me up at the airport?"

The Reverend David Master looked apprehensive. "Why, I rented it, Bishop Edwards."

"Thank goodness you didn't, at least, buy it. Do you think it suitable for a Bishop of the gospel that teaches moderation, to ride in an aircushion limousine that would be suitable for Number One, in the Kremlin, himself?"

"I . . . I . . . It never occured to me, Bishop Edwards. I was thinking of your comfort," Reverend Masters stuttered.

Mike said, "Well, in the future, consider simplicity and meekness of spirit, my characteristics rather than a yearning for creature comforts."

"Yes, Bishop Edwards."

He might as well get this young jerk under his thumb as soon as possible. If he stumbled upon something by accident, it would be easier to deal with him. But Mike decided then and there that he was going to see as few as possible of his subrodinates on this level.

They swept down Gorgi Street, the Broadway-Fifth Avenue of Moscow, and emerged into Red Square, bordering the Kremlin. Mike was quartered in the New Metropole on Sverdlov Square, only two or three blocks from the Kremlin. Even Mike Edwards who had spent the better part of the last year bringing himself up to date on Russkie progress was amazed by the extent to which they'd been able to automate a hotel.

There weren't even bellhops to take your bags to your suite. The luggage was inserted into a compartment in the reception desk, and whisked up to your rooms automatically. There was exactly one clerk at the desk, and his duties seemed largely to be those of pleasantly greeting new arrivals. Anyone who knew the ropes, could have registered himself, in the desk screens. Or, if he didn't know them, could have read the instructions in a half dozen languages.

The elevator didn't need to be operated. Its identity screen picked them up and whizzed them up to the correct floor. The Reverend Masters led the way down the corridor to the Bishop's suite, evidently having regained his confidence, since he was gushing again.

"My room adjoins your suite, Bishop Edwards. We have arranged for inter-office communication, and there is a connecting door."

"Where's Frank, uh, that is the Reverend Jones, quartered?"

"He shares your suite, sir. He thought it best that he be immediately available. You could not believe how fast things are moving. Why, we could use twice the number of missionaries we have on hand."

Mike growled, "Make a note to remind me of that, as soon as I get settled in. If we can use twice the missionaries we have on hand, we'll soon have them."

The Reverend Masters blinked. "Bishop Edwards, not that I question your word, but I sometimes wonder where all the funds come from."

Oh, oh.

Mike said severely, "Well, stop wondering. The holy message is spreading. Some of our followers are extremely wealthy. They realize the need to spread the gospel. They donate very generously."

"They must," David Masters murmured. "Bless them all. Here we are."

He opened the door and stood aside for Mike to precede him.

Mike Edwards entered and did a quick tour of the apartment. It was much the same to the one he'd had in the New Greater Washington Hotel. That is, there were two bedrooms, two baths, a large living room, complete with what he assumed to be a bar, and an office, rather larger than the one he'd had in Greater Washington. Old Frank had taste for comfort.

He returned and put himself on record. His mouth was tight.

"Is this your idea of moderation, Reverend?"

The Reverend Masters quailed. "Your Reverence, the Reverend Jones mediated at great length before coming to the conclusion that in view of the prominence of Your Reverence that it would not do to seek humble quarters. The rest of us, believe me, seek the simpler life, though it is much more difficult here in the Soviet Complex than one could dream. No one here leads what could be deemed a simple life. A hermit would be hard put to avoid champagne and caviar. It is truly most distressing. But the Reverend Jones thought it might be necessary for you to receive high officials, government authorities, for permission to continue and expand our work . . ." he let the sentence dribble away.

"I see," Mike said severely. "The Reverend Jones has been on the scene longer than I have. Undoubtedly he is more knowledgeable about local needs. I trust his sagacity implicitly. However . . ."

Mike turned and dramatically pointed at the bar.

". . . what is that?"

David Masters was in agony. "An automated bar, Your Reverence. They come in all of the suites and rooms in the New Metropole. I suggested to the Reverend Jones that we request it be removed from your quarters, but after pious deliberation he decided it was ostentatious to request alterations in our quarters. He thought, perhaps, that we could put a taptestry over it to disguise its nature."

Mike nodded curtly. "As usual, the Reverend Jones thinks out even modest problems efficiently. Now, then, Reverend, that will be all. I am weary. I shall begin activities later. Please retire. I am free to no one except the Reverend Jones."

"Yes, your Reverence, of course. I was distressed to learn that you had suffered airsickness on the way across the Atlantic. I was of the opinion that it was practically unknown on the super-sonics."

Mike said grimly, "I can get airsick just looking up at the sky on dry land. See you later, Reverend."

In actuality, the trip across had been a ball. But that was another story. Right now he could use a quick one to get him over his slight hangover. Slight, hell.

He saw the Reverend Masters to the door which joined Mike's suite to the other's room, and saw that it was well secured before heading back for his own living room and making a beeline for the bar.

The damn thing was automated. Happily, there were instructions. You could dial just about any item on a rather impressive wine and spirits list. He was just beginning to get the real hang of it when the door buzzed and the identity screen revealed the dour face of Frank Jones.

Mike let him in and they sized each other up. Both, of course, wore the somber, austere black clothing of a minister of the Old Time Religion Church, complete with reversed collar.

"Jesus," Frank Jones said. "Is this the guy who almost clobbered that whale-sized Cossack in Torremolinos?"

"I didn't know you were there that night," Mike said. "But at least I can say you look more authentic than I do."

"Like hell I do," Jones growled. "You were born to be a bishop. Let's adjourn to the bar. I had to practically slug that young jerk Masters to keep the thing in the place."

Mike remembered and raised his eyebrows and pointed to his ear. Jones stared at him for a minute, then caught on.

"Oh," he said. "No. No microphones, no secret police under the bed, nothing like that."

Mike looked at him.

Frank said reasonably. "Do you think that there's anybody more competent to check it out than I am? I'm equipped with every electronic mop put out by the Department of Dirty Tricks in the Bureau of International Investigations. The fact of the matter is, the Russkies couldn't care less what we do—just so long as we don't sound off against the government or Andrei Zorin, or any of the other top bureaucrats."

"That's what I thought," Mike said. "It's a bad sign for the West. The Russkies don't bother to have secrets any more."

He said to Frank, in front of the autobar, "What would

you like? I could become an alcoholic playing with this gadget. We ought to introduce them into the States."

"Don't think they won't," Frank said glumly. "And throw a few hundred thousand bartenders out of work. They can mix better drinks than the average bartender. Let me have pivo."

"What's a pivo?" Mike said.

"What's wrong with your Russian? Beer. Russian beer is so thick you can pit it out of your teeth, but it's better than Spanish beer."

"Anything not thick enough to eat is better to drink than Spanish beer," Mike said, dialing himself a chilled Stolitschnaja vodka. "How're things going?"

Frank Jones took a chair and knocked back an initial swallow of his drink. "Mostly we've been waiting for you to arrive. However, we've done the preliminary ground work. The country's ripe for it. Rotten ripe."

Mike found a chair too and looked at his companion, interested. "How do you know, Frank?"

The other took a pull of his beer again and scowled, looking for an example. "Well, for one thing . . . listen, do you know a character named Galushko? Nicolas Galushko?"

"Nick? Sure. He was one of my tourists in Torremolinos. The last batch I had. He was about average. He drank too much."

"Well, he doesn't any more," Frank said definitely. "He's just been making a tour through the Ukraine. Converted several thousand farm people already."

Mike stared at him. "Converted them to what?"

"Some kind of a new religion all his own. Teaches moderation. Once we get going, I think we can swing them into our organization."

"Holy smokes," Mike said, awed. He knocked back his

vodka. "I gave him the idea one night on a tapa tour through Malaga."

There came a timid knock on the door that joined the suite to the room of Reverend Masters.

Mike said, "Ditch these glasses, Frank. We don't want to louse up our images before the hired help."

Frank put the glasses in the disposal chute of the bar, and went over to the door and opened it.

It was young Masters and he had a book in his hand and puzzlement on his bland face. He had his thumb marking a page in the book.

Mike said, "What is it, son?"

"Bishop Edwards," the other said hesitantly, "Remember that Biblical quotation you gave me as we were driving from the airport?"

"Certainly."

"Well sir, I looked it up, just to be certain that I had it correctly. *Genesis* XIX. 5."

Oh, oh. He'd been caught out. He hadn't the vaguest idea what that Book, Chapter and Verse was. However, he'd have to face his subordinate down.

"Well?" he said severely.

David Masters read, "And they called to Lot and said to him, where are the men who came to you tonight? Bring them out to us so we can cornhole them."

"What!" Mike blurted.

Frank Jones went over to the Reverend Masters and took the book from his hands. "What edition of the Bible is this?"

He looked at the cover. *"The Holy Bible in Modern Idiom."* What in the devil is this all about?"

The younger man was evidently set back by his superior's vehemence. He said, looking back and forth between Frank and Mike, "It's a new edition brought out so that the present generation can understand it. The King James version sometimes confuses them."

Mike, muttering, took up his own Bible from where it had been sitting on a table. He looked up the quotation, and read: "And they called unto Lot and said unto him, Where are them which come in to thee this night? bring them out unto us, that we may know them."

"Hump," he grunted, under his breath. "I always wondered what that meant."

He put the book down again and turned severely to his assistant cum secretary. "That'll be all, Reverend Masters. I'm a busy man and don't like to be bothered with such trivials."

"Yes, Bishop Edwards." The other turned hurriedly to leave. Frank handed back to him his Bible in Idiom.

As a parting, Mike said, "One last thing, son. Verily he who holds doubts of the words of the Prophet shall come to a bitter end. *Song of Solomon*, Chapter 11, 3."

"Oh, yes, Your Reverence. How well put."

"Indeed, yes," Frank said piously.

The other baked through the door to his room, apologetically.

Frank Jones looked after him. "For Christ sakes," he said. "Do you mean to tell me that one's got an I.Q. of at least 125?" He looked at his watch. "We better get going, Mike. I've arranged for a meeting with the Minister of Culture, Alex Mikhailov."

"What for?" Mike said.

"I'll tell you on the way down," Jones said. "We've got to get TV time, and maybe get onto the newscasts. Possibly we can talk them into doing a movie about the Old Time Religion Church."

Mike let himself be led to the door. "You're getting *too* optimistic, aren't you? Why in the hell should they do a movie about us, or allow us TV time, for that matter? I doubt if they'd even sell us time."

Jones explained on the way down in the elevator. "You've got some surprises coming. You know how lousy the TV programs are back in the States? Well, they've got the same problem here. They've gone through every bag of tricks of every producer and writer and have scraped the bottom of the barrel as far as every idea is concerned."

They were in the street now, and Frank Jones pressed a button set next to the New Metropole's main entrance. In a moment, an aircushion taxi disengaged itself from the traffic flow and pulled up to the curb before them.

Mike Edwards forced himself to climb in. He was far from happy about driverless cabs. The Russkies certainly went all out in their efforts to save labor.

Jones dialed the address co-ordinates and went on with his point. "They're on an automation kick. Twenty years ago they put a million youngsters into their universities to study time and motion engineering and became automation technicians. Now they're reaping the harvest. And every time some new discovery comes along that would ordinarily toss a couple of hundred thousand people into the ranks of the unemployed, they just lower the work week for everybody in that industry. It's got down to an average of ten hours now."

"What's all that got to do with television programs?" Mike said.

Jones shrugged glumly. "In the States we've got twenty million unemployed living high on the hog on unemployment insurance and spending their time glued to the idiot box. Over here they're all supposedly employed but everybody works only ten hours a week, thirty weeks a year. The rest of the time they're looking for entertainment and the Minister of Culture in the Soviet Complex gets just as big an ulcer trying to provide his country with new TV ideas as a Madison Avenue tycoon does in our country."

Frank Jones hesitated a moment before going on. "You know, something's been building up in me ever since I got this assignment."

"Oh?" Mike said. "What?"

"I'm not so sure that there are as many differences between the West and the Soviet Complex as we usually think."

The Palace of Rest and Culture was one of the biggest eyesores in Moscow. Located on Kalugo Boulevard and immediately across from Niezkuchny Park, it dominated the skyline of this section of Moscow.

At Dobryninskaya Square Mike Edwards and Frank Jones had turned west of Gorgi Park which they paralleled on Kaluga until the Palace of Rest and Culture loomed before them.

Mike had been looking out the window of the cab at the maze of taxis and limousines that charged at headlong speed through the streets. There was something shaking to see three boisterous Russkies, often bottles in hand, carousing in the back seat of a car that had no driver. You momentarily expected disaster.

He winced as their cab seemed all but ready to crash into a brilliantly-hued driverless limousine. "Don't *any* cabs have drivers in this God forsaken town?" he complained to Jones.

"That's more of the labor saving bit," Jones said sourly. "They automated the streets so as to eliminate all the manpower formerly involved in driving the cars and then they pulled the conductors off buses and stopped selling tickets for the subways. Made all transportation free. It was wasted labor, they said, collecting fares. They've really got the bug on this wasted labor thing."

They pulled up before the skyscraper which was the entertainment center of the country and climbed from the cab. Mike slammed the door after him and the cab whizzed off into the traffic.

"Where does it all finally wind up?" he muttered, staring after the vehicle.

"Where does what wind up?" Jones said.

"This automation. Finally, they'll get it it down to where no work at all is necessary. Then what happens?"

Jones grunted. "The same thing's happening in the West. Weren't you automated out of your job?"

"Sometimes I get the feeling," Mike said, "that the human race has opened up Pandora's Box, that we've built ourselves a monster like Frankenstein never dreamed of, that we've got a Saber-Tooth tiger by the tail, that we've dropped the reins and the horse is running away with us."

"All at once?" Jones said.

"All at once," Mike said.

In the brutally large reception hall of the Palace of Rest and Culture, they spoke their piece into the screen of an auto-secretary receptionist and waited for instructions.

A voice behind them said in astonishment. "Why, it's Mike!"

They turned.

She was still unforgettably fair of skin, blue of eyes, blonde of hair, as only a northern Slav can be.

Mike said, "Catherina!"

Automatically, his eyes dropped from her face to

check, but she was wearing, by current Russkie standards, a comparatively conservative suit.

Jones cleared his throat warningly.

Mike beamed at her. "What in the world are you doing here?" he said, before she could ask him the same.

"I work here, Mike. I told you once, I think. I'm a production secretary for Bolshi-Films. But you . . . ?"

She looked at Frank, as though vaguely remembering him from Torremolinos, but then must have decided that was unlikely. Mike introduced them hurriedly and wracked his brains, not knowing exactly what to do with the situation.

Frank turned and was obtaining directions from the automatic receptionist. Now he coughed gently again and said, "Ah, we'll have to hurry."

Mike said, "Look Catherina, could I see you later? Tonight. I'll bring you up to date on what has been happening to me and why I'm here in Moscow."

"When? Where?" she said, smiling her Catherina smile at him. His stomach rolled over twice, happily.

He said, "I don't know any places. I just arrived this very day."

She thought a moment, then said, "At the cocktail bar of the Hotel Tsentralnaya, at eight."

"Wonderful," he said.

Frank said, "We should hurry," and hurry they did, Mike looking over his shoulder after the girl. Of course, she still had that fabulous set of rounded buttocks.

On the way up to the offices of Alex Mikhailov, Jones looked at him. "Who's that? I seem to have seen her somewhere before. How could you be in this town no more than a couple of hours and already have become acquainted with a broad?"

"Catherina is no broad," Mike said. "You saw her in

Torremolinos. One of the tourists," Mike added dreamily.

"And you've made a date with her to meet in a bar, eh," Frank said disgustedly.

"Ummm. Why not?"

"Remember?" Frank said accusingly. "You're a bishop of the Old Time Religion Church. You don't drink. You don't smoke. You don't dance. You don't go out with flighty looking blondes. I remember her now. She's the one that someway or other always had her tits out. But above all, you don't hang around in the most popular bar in Moscow."

"Holy smokes," Mike said. "I forgot."

"Yeah," Jones said dryly.

Mike said, "Well, Catherina Saratov is in a position to wonder how it is that a tourist guide in Southern Spain is suddenly a bishop of the Old Time Religion Church." He let his voice go thoughtful. "I suppose I'll have to spend some time with her covering up."

"Yeah," Frank said. "And obviously that's going to be one hell of a chore, so far as you're concerned. My heart is pumping piss for you."

XVII

The Interview with the Minister of Culture had been a nowling success. In fact, he had practically fallen into their arms.

After a rundown on just what it was that their Old Time Religion Church advocated, and assurances that they had nothing whatsoever to say against the Soviet Complex State and no opinions whatsoever about Russkie bureaucrats from Andrei Zorin right on down, he's practically turned over the resources of the Ministry of Rest and Culture to them.

In appearance Alex Mikhailov could have been any one of a hundred of Mike's tourist charges down on the Costa del Sol. He was big, Slavic, full of energy, gleaming of teeth, hail fellow well met, hand shaking, well—hell, lavishly—dressed, and obviously of the cream of Soviet Complex bureaucracy. If Mike had had to work under him for a month, he knew damned well he'd have ulcers, and probably D.T.s.

"Why, do you realize," he said happily, "the nearest

thing to a really new attraction we've had for six months is a dancing Panda? This calls for a celebration!" He banged happily on the bell. "Religion," he chortled. "Everybody will be overwhelmed. Something absolutely new. Who ever heard of religion?"

An underling entered from another office.

"Champagne!" Mikhailov roared. "The best Armenian vintages. Send in some of the girls from the distribution office. Dial us some food. Caviar, smoked salmon, sturgeon. Stolichny salad, Soodak fish, everything! And lots of champagne. Kirill, we're celebrating. Have the best sent in!"

Kirill was impressed. Before Mike could open his mouth, he had disappeared again.

Mike said, "But Your Excellency, we just finished telling you. The Old Time Religion Church teaches moderation."

"Yes, indeed," Jones said with a holier-than-thou tone.

"Moderation?" Alex Mikhailov said. "But a celebration is in order. Why, you'll be the hit of the season. I'll be awarded the Hero Medal for outstanding Socialist Labor. What do you mean, moderation?"

"Moderation in all things," Mike said gently. "Ostentatious display, ostentatious use of luxuries, spending one's time in such fvirolities as foreign travel, is the curse of the spiritual side of the race."

Mikhailov was flabbergasted. 'They are?" he saia blankly. "Why?"

For the next hour they told him why, fascinating him to the point that when Kirill, his secretary, returned smiling widely and heading a procession of would-be revellers, he was snarled out of the office, champagne, girls, caviar and all.

It wound up eventually with Mikhailov promising to

attend their initial meeting which was to be held in St. Basil's, the candy cane cathedral on Red Square. It was the first time the building had been used other than as a museum for generations. The Bishop's sermon was to be covered by TV and newsreel photographers.

XVIII

The interview at the Palace of Rest and Culture over, Mike hurried back to the hotel to prepare himself for his date with Catherina. He debated on whether or not to wear his clergyman clothes and then decided that he might as well stick to them. Sooner or later he was going to have to explain to Catherina that he was now a bishop.

He showered, shaved, did himself up as nattily as he could make it in black, and then impatiently waited the time out in the living room. Frank Jones had made off to finish the arrangements for the St. Basil's meeting.

Mike eyed the auto-bar thristily, but shook his head. Just as sure as hell if he took that first drink, it would be followed by more, and it wouldn't do to meet Catherina half smashed.

A knock came on the door to the Reverend Master's room, and Mike pushed the release button and growled, "Come on in."

David Masters said, "Your Reverence, I wonder if you

could spare a moment to clear me up on a point of theology."

"Why, certainly, Reverend," Mike said, being in no position to reveal that in actuality he knew about as much on theology as he did orbiting Mars. "What can it be? I understand that you were top man in your class at the seminary."

His assistant cum secretary brought his hand around from behind his back. It held a black book. He said, "Your Reverence, remember that quotation you gave me from the *Song of Solomon?* Chapter 11, 3.?"

Oh, oh. Here they went again.

"Well?"

The Reverend Masters coughed gently, apologetically, and read, "I went down on my beloved with great delight and his dong was sweet to my taste."

"What!" Mike bellowed. "Give me that book." He grabbed it. "Oh, *The Holy Bible in Modern Idiom* again, eh?" He went over to his book shelf and got his own copy.

He read, "I sat down under his shadow with great delight and his fruit was sweet to my taste."

He stared at it for a moment and muttered. "Whoever did this translation had a vivid imagination, is all I can say. In fact, a dirty mind." He read a little more of the Song of Solomon and shook his head. "On the other hand, maybe he didn't."

He put his Bible down and looked back at the Reverend Masters severely. "You must have misunderstood me. That's the wrong quotation."

"Oh, yes, sir. I was sure it was, Bishop Edwards."

"Very well, Reverend. That will be all. The next time you want to consult someone on theology, look up the Reverend Jones. I haven't time for it. And always remember, Blessed is he who performs the duties set him by his superiors without question. Two Kings XXIII 7."

"Oh, yes Your Reverence."

When the other was gone, Mike Edwards checked his watch. At long last, it was time to meet Catherina.

The cocktail bar of the Tsentralnaya was currently the most popular place in town and, when Mike Edwards first entered, the shock wave of sound generated by Russkies en masse in their cups, all but staggered him back through the door again. In Spain, at least, he'd got his Russians in no larger numbers than a couple of hundred at a time. The so-called cocktail bar must have held at least twice that, and all of them seemingly stoned, Russkie style.

He had to circle the room twice before spotting Catherina Saratov. As he made his way to her table, he tried to think what it was that was so different about her in Moscow as compared to Spain. Finally, it came to him. Catherina was absolutely conservative, compared to the others in the room. And then he realized that she was undoubtedly dressed in the Old-Fashioned Look fashion.

He sat down across from her wordlessly, let his eyes take her in with complete enjoyment. The fact that she was doing the same, was obviously as pleased with his presence as he was with hers, didn't lessen the enjoyment.

Somehow they had no immediate need to speak. They both knew that this was it and that something wonderful would come of it all. Something very wonderful.

Mike opened his mouth at last but the blast of sound which surrounded them all but drowned out his words.

He shouted to her, "Why did you suggest that we meet here?"

She shouted back, "I wanted you to see it."

"Why?" he shouted.

She stood, put a hand on his arm and led him towar the entry.

In the lobby, Mike shook his head for clarity. "Hol smokes," he said. "I used to think all bars were essential ly the same. Evidently Moscow has exceptions to offe Can't we go somewhere and talk?"

"Of course. Do you like Georgian cuisine? The Aragv restaurant, over on Gorki Street, is comparatively quiet."

"Anything is comparatively quiet to that place i there."

She chuckled. "We Russians have several generation of—what is your term?—*living-it-up* to catch up with."

Mike said, "In spite of the success of your speed-u projects in other fields, I wonder about this one."

Catherina laughed. "We shall have to make a ne Seven Year Plan."

Mike gestured at the bar they'd just left. "They seen to want to accomplish it in seven weeks. Why did yo say you wanted me to see that place?"

"I'll tell you when we get to the Aragvi."

The Aragvi was located at 6 Gorki Street, only a fe steps off Revolution Place. It turned out to be one of th older top restaurants in the Russkie capital. Mike an Catherina got as far away from the orchestra as possibl and Mike dialed a bottle of Teliani.

However, when the bottle came, Catherina shook he head as he began to pour. "I'm not drinking these days It ties in with my reason for wanting you to see that ter rible bar—just as an example. Actually, I haven't forgot ten what you said in Malaga. Mike, what is happening t my people?"

He twirled his glass in his fingers. They had arrived a

the point where it looked as though he was going to have to go into his act. He hated the idea. This was Catherina. He didn't want any falseness between them.

Mike said slowly, "You touched on it earlier when you were joking about catching up on your living-it-up. With that series of five-year and seven-year plans you people went through for so long, you accumulated a head of steam. Now you're blowing it." He didn't add, *and in so doing are fouling the economies of the rest of the world.*

Catherina said, "Until a year ago, I was part of it. Nothing seemed to make much difference excepting to have a good time. Now, Mike, I'm afraid. Look at us. No ambition except to attend another party, to over-drink, over-play, to go to bed with whoever's available. Twenty years or so ago we had our *mitrofanushka*, our *stilyagi.* What is it in America?"

"Juvenile delinquents."

"Yes," she nodded. "Practically everybody was contemptuous of them. We expected our youth to study, to work hard, to help build out country to the point where it was as strong as any."

"And so you did," Mike said, keeping the sour quality from his voice.

"Yes, and now what? Pride in study or work is a thing of the past. Everybody has become *stilyagi.* Even our adults are delinquent."

Mike said uncomfortably. "What are you building up to, Catherina?"

She leaned across the table and touched his hand. "Mike, what you were telling us about the need to devote yourself to higher things than dulling your God-given senses with alcohol and over-indulgence. Mike, our people have to be given this message."

Mike sat back in his chair and blinked at her. For the

first time it occurred to him that far from pulling a gimmick out of the Bag of Dirty Tricks for the benefit of the West, he was sponsoring a program that ultimately was more needed by the Russkie side than by his own.

She twisted her mouth ruefully. "But then, I don't suppose you wanted to see me this evening to have laid in your lap the problems of the Soviet Complex. Let's talk about us, Mike."

He moistened suddenly dry lips. "Yes," he said. "Let's talk about us."

XIX

"Not quite yet," she said. "First we order dinner. I don't want a famished man on my hands." Her blue eyes went wicked. "You'll want your strength, later on. Every bit of it."

His belly did a flip-flop. He was under her spell again, already. He said, "You're the boss. You do the ordering. I'm not up on Russian food to any extent."

She took up the menu and looked at it. She said, "Zakouski?"

"I beg your pardon?"

Catherina laughed at him. "Zakouski are the Russian equivalent of hors d'oeuvres. Cavair, both black and red, is an example. They're salty and spicy and have the reputation of being aphrodisical. Hmmm." She looked mischievous.

Mike said, "We'll have Zakouski."

She looked back at the menu. "And, since this is a Georgian restaurant, we should have shashlik. That comes out lumps of spiced mutton skewered on a dagger.

And we can wind it all up with saluguni, a Georgia cheese which is best served hot."

"You're the boss," he repeated.

The Aragvi Restaurant, evidently in attempt to kee its decor of yesteryear, was only partially automatec One could dial drinks and wine and have them delivere through the table top, but the waiters were live. Cath erina summoned one and gave the order and then lai the menu back on the table.

Mike wanted a drink somewhat desperately, an poured himself a meagre half glass of the wine.

She said, "And did you take the Holy Orders you tol me about in Torremolinos?"

"Well, yes."

There were the two faint lines about her clear eye She said, "But you still drink?"

"In moderation," he told her. "The Old Time Religio Church teaches moderation, not necessarily abstinence It was Saint Paul who said, '. . . use a little wine for th stomach's sake.' "

Catherina was mildly surprised. "He did? Well, the I'll join you."

He poured for her, filling her glass, and then his own If he was going to be seeing this girl of his fondes dreams, he was going to have to make some amendment to some of the things he had told her. He wanted woman, not a nun.

He said, "For instance, we teach moderation in eating An obese person is ruining his God-given body. But w do not teach starvation, or even fasting. One must ea well to remain healthy."

"Why, that certainly makes sense," she said, taking sip from her glass.

The Zakouski came and for a few minutes they busied themselves with it.

Mike said, trying to get back into a lighter vein. "I can feel it working already."

She looked at him. "What working?"

"You said Zakouski had an aphrodisiac effect."

"Oh, you fool," she laughed. Then she said, "I see you are dressed in the Old-Fashioned Look style. It's beginning to sweep the Soviet Complex. Is that collar one of the latest in men's wear in America?"

Mike Edwards touched his reversed collar self-consciously. He hated the damn thing. He said, "Not exactly. You see, I'm a bishop of the Old Time Religion Church. All of our ministers dress like this."

"A bishop!" she exlaimed. "How wonderful. How hard you must have had to work to gain such a rank so quickly."

"Well, yes," he said, playing it modest. "You'd be surprised the number of people I had to work."

In actuality, damn it, he still had certain qualms about deceiving her. But, then, *was* he deceiving her? He had already won his battle with his conscience in so far as introducing this new religion to the Russkies, and Catherina herself had only a short time again told him how badly the Soviet Complex needed the teachings.

He was a touch surpried, by the time they had finished their meal, to find that they had finished the bottle of wine as well. There was a faint flush on her face, which only improved her perfect complexion. Evidently, Catherina hadn't been doing much drinking in the recent past and was unused to it.

She said, "Should we go to my apartment? If I'm not mistaken, I have put away, somewhere or other, a half bottle of cognac. I haven't touched it for ages, but I don't believe brandy spoils in the bottle, does it?" Her face went mischievous again. "It seems to me that on another occasion I invited you to my hotel suite for a final drink."

He summoned the waiter for his bill with considerably more elan than befitted a bishop.

Out on the street, they strolled down to the corner to a public phone screen where she summoned an aircushion cab, and stood there waiting for it.

But before it arrived a voice roared. "Mike! Mike Edwards, what are you doing in Moscow?"

Mike winced, but turned to face he who bellowed. It was, of all people, Vovo Chernozov, who promptly embraced the American in a bear hug that all but broke ribs. All over again, Mike wondered how he'd ever gotten through that evening in Torremolinos with this monster.

But, "Vovo!" Mike and Catherina said simultaneously.

The overgrown Cossack pushed Mike back, the better to look at him, but still held onto his shoulders. He took in the reversed collar in surprise. "Then you are . . . ?"

Catherina said, "Mike has become the Bishop Michael Edwards of the Old Time Religion Church, Vovo. You'll remember him telling us about it in Spain."

"A bishop!" Vovo exclaimed. He took up Mike's hand and kissed it, Russian fashion. "May I have your blessings, Your Reverence? I too am of the faith. I took my vows last week in Kharkov."

Holy smokes, Mike thought inwardly. What next? Vovo a member of the Old Time Religion Church. He had never given anyone his blessings before, and hadn't the vaguest idea how to go about it. But, what the hell, he was a bishop wasn't he?

"May God preserve you, my son," he said with priestly unction.

"Thank you, Your Reverence," Vovo gushed. "It was only last week. Reverend Matheson, who is a graduate of your seminary in America, came to the city to spread the gospel. I attended the first sermon and was immediately converted, with many others. He continues to spread the Holy word. Moderation in all things. He is a Saint!"

Mike Edwards began to blurt, *Matheson a saint!* but controlled himself. Instead, he said, "Vovo, my son, there are no saints in the Old Time Religion Church. Or, perhaps, I should say, each of us are saints in our own way if we rigidly adhere to the gospel."

The aircushion taxi that Catherina had summoned smoothed up the to the curb beside them and the door opened automatically.

She said to Vovo, hesitantly, "I didn't even know you were in town."

He beamed at her. "I would have looked you up, and Ana Chekova as well. She too has been received into the bosom of the Church. But I am here on Old Time Religion affairs, getting permission to renovate our church."

Catherina said, still hesitantly, "Mike . . . that is, the bishop, and I were about to go to my apartment to talk over old times . . . and religious matters, of course. Why don't you come along, Vovo? Undoubtedly, it would be very inspiring."

He loked devastated. "I cannot. I have to catch my plane back to Kharkov."

Mike said cautiously, "Renovate your church?"

Vovo was very happy about it. "Yes. Tomorrow I am to wrestle—Turkoman style, of course—at a great sports exhibition. If I win the prize, it will go to the renovation of an old church from Czarist times, now in semi-ruin. All the members of the congregation have wagered their life savings on me. What they win will also go into the fund. Then the Old Time Religion will have a church—well, it was formerly a cathedral—of its own in Kharkov. Already we are pressed for space to accommodate those who come to hear the message of moderation."

Mike felt like turning his eyes up, but he had to play his part. He said severely, "My son, Vovo, gambling is not the practice of the simple, meek, life."

"Gambling!" Vovo said indignantly. "Wagering on my victory is not gambling, Your Reverence. It is a sure thing."

Bishop Edwards shook his head. "It is not my practice to interefere with the activities of a local congregation. Reverend Matheson is on the scene. If he had condoned this, then you have my blessings. I am sure the Lord will see that you are victorious."

"Amen," Catherina said, somewhat sarcastically. "Remember what he did to that poor bull in Malaga?"

Mike could have added, "And what he did to me in La Manana?" but refrained.

Vovo said, "I must go. Another time, Your Reverence. Another time, Catherina." He looked at her. "You are a member of the Faith?"

Catherina looked at Mike. She said, "I haven't as yet taken my vows. The bishop is kind enough to be instructing me."

Vovo shot a look at his watch. "I must be off." He looked Mike squarely in the eyes. "Moderation in all things!" he intoned.

Mike answered in the set formula. "May all enjoy the simple blessed pleasures of the home and family and not wander away from it in vain seeking of far pleasures, my son."

My son, yet, he thought inwardly. It would have taken an elephant to have fathered Vovo Chernozov. He felt inward sympathy however, for the victim who was going to fight the Cossack, Turkoman style, in Kharkov on the morrow.

The other was off, hurriedly.

Catherina and Mike climbed into the cab and she dialed directions.

On the way to her apartment, she said quietly, "Vovo was quite inspiring, Mike. What are the requirements for joining the Old Time Religion Church?"

Oh, oh. Here we go. He didn't like this at all. This was Catherina.

Mike said, "That you be a member of the human race, Catherina Saratov, and that you abide by the gospel. Nothing more than that."

"And suppose that in my time I have slept with a good many men, drank a good deal, was seldom . . . moderate. Even experimented with some of the less difficult narcotics?"

"Catherina," he said, "the Old Time Religion Church is not interested in your past. It is interested in your present and in your future. All of us, before finding the Old Time Religion, have sinned . . . have been less than adequate."

Holy smokes, he thought, how hypocritical can you get? But then it came back to him all over again. She herself had said it. What the Soviet Complex needed was exactly what he was delivering. But then, all over again, his conscience hit him. The Machiavellian creed: the end justifies the means. But does it? His ends were those of the West. Were they those of Catherina, Vovo and Ana Chekova, and all the rest?

And then he had still second thoughts. Perhaps they were.

Catherina's apartment building was automated as everything seemed to be automated in Moscow. There was no doorman, no reception desk, no elevator operator, and when they approached the door of her apartment the identity screen picked her up and the door swung open.

The apartment itself was *lived in.* It had the feeling of a home, rather than just a sterile flat. It was well done, nothing of the garish moderninity of some of the apartments, flats and houses with which Mike was all too familiar in the States. It was *Catherina.*

She tossed her shoulder bag to a table and said, "As you Americans say—at least, so I've heard, you say—make yourself at home. I'll try and find my bottle of cognac. I haven't the vaguest idea of where it is."

While she was gone, he wandered over to her bookcase and inspected the writings she evidently valued. They were almost all good books. More than half were nonfiction. Those that were fiction were good writers, and Russian novelists didn't predominate. She had catholic tastes. The French, British and Americans were well represented. His respect for Catherina Saratov grew. She was not just an ultra-shaped broad on a Spanish beach, topless.

By the time she had returned, bottle of brandy in hand, and two glasses, he had decided, all over again, that this was the woman he loved.

She set him back, after pouring the two glasses and sitting herself across from him, by leaning forward, her slight frown above her eyes, and saying, "Mike, do you believe in this religion of yours?"

Oh, oh. This was the woman he loved—hadn't he just told himself?

He set down the glass he had taken up and thought about it. He said finally, "Catherina, perhaps the more one knows about one's religion, the less one believes. And I suspect that this applied down through the ages."

She took a fairly major swallow of her own drink. "Then you don't believe in what you teach?"

"No, it's not that." He worried it. "I do believe in the basic tenents of the Old Time Religion. That is, I believe in moderation, in being humble, in the more simple life. I believe in the virtues, if that is the term, of family life, of loving one's close relatives—unless they are not loveable, of course—and one's neighbors."

"So do I," she said softly.

Mike took a deep breath. "However, I have my doubts about there being supreme powers that are guiding our destinies."

"So do I," she said, taking another sip of her brandy. "And that's one of the reasons I've wondered about you, Mike. I love you, but I wonder about you. You are a very intelligent man. Forgive me, but I've had you checked out. You are a well known political economist with an Academician's degree, which is no easier to take in America than it is in the Soviet Complex. It sounds like a silly thing to say, but, Mike, I suspect you're one of the smartest men in the United States."

He looked at her in agony.

She took another of her mild sips of brandy and said, "Mike, are you here to hurt my people?"

He took a slug of the brandy himself.

She said urgently, "Would you hurt Vovo and Ana?"

He closed his eyes wearily. She was the woman he

loved. He was able to say, finally, "No, Catherina, of course I wouldn't hurt Vovo nor Ana . . . nor you."

"Then what are you doing? You are not religious. You are an outstanding socioeconomist. What are you doing in the Soviet Coplex?"

In all the world there were exactly four persons who knew what he was doing in the Soviet Complex; he, himself, Frank Jones, the President of the United States and Lawrence Bigelow' Director of the Bureau of International Investigations.

He said, "I am here to teach moderation, the simple life, meekness, and especially the desirability of remaining at home to enjoy one's family, relations and friends."

She looked at him keenly and it came to Mike Edwards that the woman he loved was far from a fool.

"Rather than traveling abroad and, ah, living it up, eh?" she said.

"Yes."

"Why does the American government– I assume this is backed by the American government, since it is obviously an expensive matter. Why does your government object to Russians traveling abroad?"

"It's not just the Americans. It's the whole West. Soviet Complex tourism is destroying its economy. You see, to support your tourism you dump your automation produced manufactured products on the world market, stifling the trade of America and all the rest. We can't compete when you sell typewriters for ten dollars, when one of those new Mikoyan cameras goes for peanuts, when sports equipment such as that new TV fishing rod that Nick Galushko had in Torremolinos is practically given away."

"I see," she said, sipping at her cognac thoughtfully.

"So there you have it," Mike told her. "If we could just

cut the tide of Soviet Complex dumping for a year or so, we might get underway again. Cutting down tourism is the answer—we hope."

She looked at him. "Perhaps if the economies of the West are so weak that they fall into depression under such pressure, they deserve to fall, to be replaced by something better. Have you considered that?"

He said wearily, "No, I have not seriously considered that, Catherina. For better or for worse, I am working for the status quo in my country."

She sighed and said, "Very well, you have honestly confided in me. I won't betray you." She put her glass down and said, "But this is not the reason we came here, is it . . . darling?"

What was it about the girl that made his throat tighten every time he thought of her as a woman.

She came to her feet, and he to his and she preceeded him to the bedroom, not exactly demurely.

She said, over her shoulder, her own voice husky, "This is disgraceful. It's not even dark as yet."

He couldn't think of any answer to that. As a matter of fact, there wasn't any answer.

In the bedroom she turned to him and put her arms around his neck.

"Kiss me, the way you kissed me in Torremolinos, that night before I left," she murmured.

He kissed her the way he had kissed her the night before she left. And then some.

All of a sudden they realized that their clothes were terribly in the way, and began to fumble out of them. Fumble was the only word; they were so hurried that fingers and thumbs seemed terribly clumsy.

The room was quite light, so that he could enjoy the beauty of her lush, not too lush, figure. She closed her eyes, lying on her back, her legs slightly spread, as he first fondled then kissed her magnificent breasts. The nipples rose in response to his caress.

He ran a hand down over her body, over her belly.

She said, "I can't . . . I can't wait. Take me darling." She fumbled for his erection, took it eagerly into her hand.

He had wanted a pillow under her, the way they had done it the first time, but that would have taken too long. Split seconds were too long. She parted her legs further, bent her knees to receive him, and guided his man-organ to the threshhold of her body.

She sighed deeply when he entered and again when she held the full length of his shaft. She wrapped her heels behind him so that they fit in the cavity behind his knees and moved in perfect unison.

So aroused was Catherina that she came to orgasm almost immediately. He tried to hold his back, so that she could come again, and was successful to the point that she'd had two climaxes before his own could be restrained any further. They finished together in a blaze of fulfillment.

For long moments they lay there, still together, and for a time he thought that possibly he could continue without rest.

But then he rolled away and over onto his back.

She said, "And so, Bishop Edwards, this is what you call moderation."

Mike laughed, though he was still breathing deeply from the orgasm. He said, "Of course. The Old Time Religion is not opposed to sex, in moderation. It is the most beautiful thing in life. What it doesn't approve of is promiscuity. There should be love before sex. So let that be a lesson to you, young woman. If you have another boy friend, you're going to have to ditch him."

"I have no other man at this time, Mike," she said softly. "You are my only man." She added wickedly, "How many times can you do it in one day and still call it sex in moderation?"

"Hmmm," he said. "We'll see."

She reached over to grasp him intimately, to arouse him to further passion.

"That we will," she said.

XX

From the first, it went with shocking success. For every flow of tide there is ebb and the hedonistic tidal wave that had engulfed the Russkies was at its crest when Mike Edwards' missionaries struck.

Overnight, the reversal to conservatism in dress, in cars, in entertainment, took place.

In lectures, in revivals, in church meetings, on TV, the message was spread. Bolshi-Films did a score of quickie movies. A hundred theatrical groups produced plays. Clubs were formed, organizations sprung up. All to promote the new belief. Moderation was the new Russkie fad. Nowhere can a fad spread so rapidly as through a people with time on their hands—and in all history there had never been a people with so much time on hand as the automation-freed Russians.

It was some six months later, two o'clock in the morning, and Mike Edwards was comfortably asleep in his suite at the New Metropole when the banging came at the door. Frank Jones was away on an evangelistic tour of the Crimea.

Mike rolled over, tried to ignore it, clung desperately to his dream of married life with Catherina. Finally he swung his feet over the bed's side, growling, "There's a bell, damn it. Don't break the door down."

There were two of them and they pushed by him and into the living room of the suite. They were six-footers, two hundred pounders, empty of expression, inconspicuous of clothing. Yes, and the flat of feet.

Actually, since the Aeroflot rocketplane had landed him at Vnukovo airport, Mike had expected them, sooner or later.

However, he began, "What is the meaning of——"

One of them said, "Get dressed."

Mike said, "I want to call the American Embassy."

They grunted amusement in unison at that, as though they had been rehearsed. They followed him into the bedroom and watched impassionately as he dressed.

Mike said, "I demand to be allowed to phone the American Embassy."

"No phone calls," one said.

There was nobody in the halls of the New Metropole at this time of night. They descended by the elvator, hustled through the lobby and into a large black limousine, for once one with a chauffeur.

One of his bulky escorts sat to the right of Mike Edwards, the other to the left. They said nothing, in full character.

At this point, Mike told himself sourly, I should have a little glass capsule of cynanide hidden in my mouth. Wasn't that the way they did it in the old days? Mike had few illusions about the ability of the Russkies to break him down under pressure.

And just when the effects of the campaign had been showing results.

They by-passed Red Square and skirted the Alexandrovsk Sad park along the west side of the Kremlin. They entered at the Borovitskij Gate, went up the cobblestoned incline there without loss of pace and drew up before the Bolshoi Kremlevski Dvorets, the Great Kremlin Palace.

Two sentries snapped to attention as they entered. Evidently, Mike's guards needed no passes. A sixteen-step ornate staircase led them up from the ground floor to a gigantic vestibule the vault of which was supported by four monolithic granite columns. They turned left and entered an anteroom. There were more guards here who also sprang to the salute.

One of Mike's escorts approached a heavy door and knocked discreetly. Someone came, opened it slightly, evidently said something to someone back in the room, and then opened it widely enough for Mike and his guards.

The chamber had obviously once been a Czarist reception room. Now it was a not overly large office. Mike stood a dozen feet from the door and looked at the man behind the desk, who, in turn, looked at him.

There was no doubt about who it was. Andrei Zorin, the fourth generation dictator of the Soviet Complex. The heir of Lenin, Stalin, Khrushchev, and so on, down the decades. Number One, Chairman of the Presidium of the Central Committee.

Zorin was a man of fifty odd, heavy-set, frowzy, a weary disillusionment about his tired eyes. His character, so far as the outside world knew, was largely a mystery. A reversal from the exhibitionism of some of his predecessors, such as Nikita Khrushchev. In more than twenty years of authority he'd never granted an inter-view to western journalists, a fact that hadn't endeared him.

Number One leaned back in his chair. He said in Rus-sian, "Frol, Kliment, you may leave." The two guards turned and left the room.

There was only one other left now with Mike and Zorin, a younger man, as thin and nervous as Zorin was heavy and stolid.

Zorin said, "This is Nuritdin Kirichenko, Minister of Internal Security."

In other words, Mike told himself, head of the secret police.

Zorin said, "Sit down, Mr. Edwards."

Mike shrugged and took a heavy leather chair. He might as well enjoy what relaxation he could at this point. He had no illusions about the future.

Zorin said, "I understand that your Russian is fluent so if you have no objections we'll speak my language. My English is atrocious."

"No objections," Mike said. He had a mouse-being-played-with feeling, although Zorin was more like a moth-eaten bear than a cat.

Zorin picked up a paper from the desk before him, put on a pair of reading glasses, and read. "Michael J. Ed-wards, Academician degree in political economy in your early twenties." He looked up at Mike, over the top of his steel-rimmed glasses. "Congratulations. Quite an accom-plishment, so I understand."

"Thanks," Mike said.

Zorin went back to his report. "Spent some years teaching political economy as a professor in the Universi-ty of New Mexico. Resigned and took position as tourist agent in Spain. Eventually began an association with a

Mr. Frank Jones, notoriously ah, hatchetman, I believe the Western term is, for the anti-Soviet Complex organization the Bureau of International Investigation, for the time working under the anti-Soviet Complex organization NATO. Returned to America for a series of secretive meetings with top Western officials such as the President and Lawrence Bigelow. Emerged in approximately a year as a high official of the . . ." Zorin squinted at his paper again ". . . the Old Time Religion Church. A religious organization of which we can find no previous record. Six months ago, arrived in Moscow and with a large staff began a strenuous and highly expensive program to spread the new faith."

Zorin looked up at Mike, and leaned back in his swivel chair.

Mike Edwards said nothing. He had passed the point of despair where anything made any difference. He only wished that they'd had as little as one more month to work. By then nothing would have stopped them.

Zorin said, "Frankly, from the first we couldn't understand what in the world you had in mind."

Mike said, "From the first!"

Kirichenko, who up until this time hadn't opened his mouth, doing nothing more than remaining on his chair and jittering nervously, said, "Did you think us fools? We of the Party have had the better part of a century's experience in international intrigue."

That was a good question, Mike decided.

Zorin quieted his colleague with a tired sweep of his hand. He said, "We were, frankly, intrigued. We must thank you for an interesting puzzle to solve."

Mike reached hopefully for a straw. "There is no puzzle. My organization is simply evangelizing its faith."

"Of course," Zorin said, not even bothering to use a

sarcastic note. He picked up another paper. "We sa
light as Soviet exports fell off and, unsurprisingly, thos
of the United States and Common Market all began t
grow."

Mike forgot about the straw. They had him all righ
He supposed that Frank Jones and the others were eve
now being corralled. He wondered how stringent th
measures taken against the Russkies who had joined u
would be. People like Vovo and Ana. He felt a twinge o
fear for Catherina. Catherina! They had planned to b
married shortly. Even though in this day and age, fe
couples bothered to go through the formalities any more.

Zorin tossed the paper back to his desk. He looked a
Mike again, appraisingly.

He said, "You did an excellent job, Mr. Edwards. It i
my despair that we of the Soviet Complex have so fe
young men, any more, who care about doing an excellen
job. They are more fond of having an excellent time.'

Mike shrugged. He wondered momentarily if it'd b
worth the try to jump the desk and try to use a littl
karate on Number One. Would the pure pleasure of get
ting in just one or two blows be worth the extra wokrin
over they'd undoubtedly give him?

Zorin said interestedly, "Do you think it will work?"

Mike brought his attention back to reality. "Do I thin
what will work?"

Number One was impatient. "Your idea of teachin
moderation with the long distance view of minimizin
Soviet Complex tourism and eventually reviving Wester
trade as our own falls off?"

Mike snorted in self-deprecation. Why kid around an
longer? They knew the whole story. "I originally hope
that it would. Now, obviously, you've caught me."

"That's not what I asked you," Zorin said, only slightly impatient. "Do you think it will work?"

Mike stared at him.

Zorin spelled it out. "Thus far, Mr. Edwards, we have taken no steps to prevent your organization from continuing its efforts." He looked over at his Minister of Internal Security. "In fact, Comrade Kirichenko, here, is in favor of my joining the Old Time Religion Church to set an example."

It took several moments for that to be assimilated. Mike said finally, "Look, have you got a drink around here?"

Zorin chuckled as he brought a bottle from the desk. "My dear Bishop Edwards, remember? Moderation?" He brought out three large shot glasses, poured the yellowish liquid into them. "Moskovskaya Starka vodka," he said. "The best, flavored with forest herbs."

Mike knocked the drink, stiff-wristed, back over his palate.

The two Russkies joined him, solemnly. Zorin poured three more. "This should really be served ice cold," he said.

Mike said, "Look, could we start somewhere nearer to the beginning?"

Number One scowled at him. "Frankly, I'm not sure where the beginning is. Maybe with Lenin. Vladimir Ilyich Ulyanov's main task was to bring the Bolsheviks to power. He succeeded. Stalin's main task was to pacify the country under Party rule and to lay the foundations for industrialization. He succeeded. The jobs of Khrushchev and Brezhnev were to overtake the West in production. They succeeded. My job has been to automate and computerize Soviet Complex production to the point of outstripping the West. I have succeeded." Zorin looked at Mike, an expression on his heavy face. "But I am not sure that it all of my task. You are a scholar of political economy, Mr. Edwards. What would you say?"

Mike was gaining courage by the minute. He said, "Well, according to your boy, Karl Marx, once the revolution was successful, the State was going to wither away. Instead, ever since Lenin's time, you've been strengthening it."

Zorin said, interestedly, "Did it ever occur to you, Mr. Edwards, that handing over power isn't the simplest thing in the world? We of the Central Committee admittedly govern the Soviet State today. To whom would we hand over our power?"

Mike was momentarily stopped. "Well," he said, "to the people. Let them democratically elect their own officials."

Number One was scowling again. "Revoutions don't come from the top down, Mr. Edwards. They come from the bottom up. And they have in the past through the efforts of a frustred majority, often a starving one, been pushed by economic necessity to overthrow their ruling class. Where is the starving majority in the Soviet Complex today? A few decades ago the Yugoslavian Djilas railed against the New Class that was growing in the Soviet countries. But as time passed more and more of our people graduated into that class. Now they're all members."

Mike said frowning, "You mean you wish you could step down, and can't.

Kirichenko said nervously, "When men in power let go the reins, things have a way of getting out of hand. None of us looks forward to the possibility of some hotheads lining us up against the nearest wall or hanging us by the heels from a handy lamppost."

Zorin said unhappily, "Actually, there is no one to hand our power. No one is interested in taking it. No one could care less." He sighed deeply. "I come back to my earlier question, Mr. Edwards. Do you think it will work?"

"You mean the new religion?" Mike couldn't quite get the others' lack of antagonism. "Well, so far it has, and it's growing fast."

Zorin said, "Maybe it's the answer. I don't know."

"Answer to what?" Mike said, all but snappishly. He'd come a long way in confidence since entering this office twenty minutes before.

Zorin was staring at him. "Maybe you of the West can help," he muttered. "Perhaps its our only chance. Perhaps we can enlarge upon your idea. Bring a new spark of life to . . ." He let his sentence fade off unhappily.

Kirichenko came to his feet, reached over and poured the three of them still another drink. The bottle was getting low. He said, "Let's get down to the essentials. If we're going to discuss this with a representative of the West, we might as well put our cards on the table." He added sourly, "They aren't very high cards."

This just didn't make sense. Mike Edwards had come to Moscow with the feeling that the West was up against the wall and his job was to make a feeble attempt to escape the situation the Soviet Complex had them in. But the way these two were talking, you'd think the positions were reversed.

Zorin said, "To sum it up, Mr. Edwards, you of the United States and the rest of the Western countries have been stymied in your economies."

Mike rasped, "Because of forty million Russian tourists spilling over your borders each year, and with every chance of the number growing."

"Forty million," Kirichenko grunted bitterly. "Nothing!"

"Nothing?" Mike said indignantly.

The Soviet Complex's number one bureaucrat sighed. "Mr. Edwards," he said, "have you noticed the rather large number of Chinese about Moscow?"

"Why yes. You mean the students, the trade delegations, the cultural exhcnage artists?"

"Ha," Kirichenko said bitterly, reaching for his drink.

"I mean the tourists," Zorin said. "They're just beginning." He ran a hand over his face wearily. "There were fifty million of them this year. Chinese—finally successful in their Great Leaps Forward—keen to begin seeing the world. And where do they most want to go? To Russia! The fatherland of communism. Every good communist in China wants to see Moscow, Leningrad, the Crimea and so forth. Their aircraft factories are working under forced draft to provide air liners for the traffic. It is estimated that the number will be one hundred million next year, two hundred the year following. Mr. Edwards, do you realize that the present population of China exceeds a billion?"

Mike was taken aback.

He said slowly, "You mean that you too would like to figure out some way of keeping the tourists out of your country. But . . ." he thought about it. ". . . you haven't the same problem we have. You don't need foreign trade. Why not just let them come?"

Zorin spelled it out for him, his face desperate. "Mr. Edwards, the Chinese have had one famed attribute down through history. Their ability to swallow up the invader. China would be overrun and conquered by an enemy. A few decades later the enemy would have interbred with the hundreds of millions of Chinese; a century later there would be no signs of the enemy left."

Mike said, "What's this got to do with tourism?"

"Isn't it obvious? Here, have another drink. Kirichenko get out another bottle. Mr. Edwards, as you've undoubtedly noticed, Russian morals have loosened considerably in the past generation. In the early days of Bolshevik power we were actually quite puritanical, absolutely Victorian in our sexual code. But, as you've undoubtedly seen, as our people become more hedonistic, the moral code slips."

Mike was gaping at him, comprehension beginning to dawn.

"Two hundred or three hundred million Chinese," Zorin shuddered, "crossing our borders on pleasure bent, each year. Estimate, Mr. Edwards. With our present loose sexual code, how long do you think it would be before there wasn't a full-blooded Russian left in the country?" His voice dropped to an anguished whisper. "How long before there weren't any Russians left at all? It was a sad day when we patched up the difficulties we had with China back during Brezhnev's times."

Kirichenko was pouring another round, his hand shaking.

Mike said, "Holy smokes, and then when they'd all seen Russia thoroughly, they'd start in seeing the rest of the world."

"Exactly," Zorin said emphatically. He came to his feet, weaving only a trifle.

"Mr. Edwards," he said incisively, "to use an old Americanism, let's face it. The cold war is over between us. Not in an Armageddon, not in a Gotterdammerung of guided missiles and H-Bombs, but in the face of a problem common to both."

Mike and Kirichenko came to their own feet, their faces set firmly, their glasses upraised.

Mike bit out courageously, slurring only slightly, "The common enemy of all," he toasted. "Tourists! They must and shall be stopped!"